And Then there Was Us

KERN CARTER

And Then there Was Us

tundra

Tundra Books, an imprint of Tundra Book Group,
a division of Penguin Random House of Canada Limited

*Publisher's note: This book is a work of fiction. Names, characters, places and
incidents either are the product of the author's imagination or are used
fictitiously, and any resemblance to actual persons living or dead,
events, or locales is entirely coincidental.*

Library and Archives Canada Cataloguing in Publication

Title: And then there was us / Kern Carter.
Names: Carter, Kern, author.
Identifiers: Canadiana (print) 20230150306 | Canadiana (ebook) 20230150322 |
ISBN 9781774883402 (hardcover) | ISBN 9781774883419 (EPUB)
Classification: LCC PS8605.A777825 A85 2024 | DDC jC813/.6—dc23

Published simultaneously in the United States of America by Tundra Books
of Northern New York, an imprint of Tundra Book Group,
a division of Penguin Random House of Canada Limited

Library of Congress Control Number: 2023930957

Edited by Lynne Missen
Jacket designed by Gigi Lau
Typeset by Griffin Hajek
The text was set in Minion Pro

Printed in Canada

www.penguinrandomhouse.ca

1 2 3 4 5   28 27 26 25 24

Penguin
Random House
tundra | TUNDRA BOOKS

February

TODAY IS THE DAY I'VE BEEN EXPECTING FOR FOUR years, seven months and twenty-four days. I put my hand over my heart to catch it from sinking and let the phone ring out while staring at the screen. Mommy? Why does my screen say mommy? There's no way I'm ready to hear her voice. No way I'm ready to listen to what she has to say.

My dad is moving stuff into storage today, so it's just me, sitting in my room with my headphones on drawing on my iPad. My phone is on the floor beside me, still lit from the missed call. I'm waiting to see if there's any text notification, one of those long, essay-type messages I'd have to scroll through to read her explanation for where she was when I graduated middle school, or what she was doing when I got my driver's license, or why she wasn't there to scream at me when I smoked weed for the first time, got my nose pierced and dyed my hair blond.

I don't know why I'm acting like this. I told myself a million times that I'm over this whole having a mom thing. And I am. I really am. Never mind that her number is still saved as Mommy in my phone and seeing that word

3

splashed across my screen triggers all this bullshit I spent years dealing with.

She calls again. Mommy. And it's like the vibration from the phone is echoing through my body. I'm staring at the red Cancel icon knowing what I should do, but I lower my headphones and swipe green to answer.

"Hi."

My first words. Our first words since not long after I got my period. I put my iPhone to my ear and cover my other ear with my finger to keep it all in. Even the walls in my room feel like intruders, so even though I'm home alone, when I say "hi," it comes out just above a whisper.

"Hello, Coi." Her voice sounds restrained, almost calm, and still has the melodic tone I remember so well. I wait for what's next. What words are going to come out of her mouth? "How are you?"

"Good."

"You sound good."

"Thanks."

"Are you busy?"

"No."

"What are you doing?"

"Nothing."

My mother was never comfortable with silence. I can still hear 50 Cent and Jay-Z and Beres Hammond and Buju Banton blaring at all times of the day and night. The only thing louder than the music was her screaming at me to do some chore or yelling at her boyfriend over the phone. It was either that or her laughing at one of the Housewives shows, usually Atlanta, like she had the same condition as the Joker, and getting so into it that she'd jump on the couch and turn the volume all the way up.

"Nothing?" she repeats. I don't respond. "I really miss you, Coi."

"Okay."

"Okay? That's it?"

"What do you want me to say?"

"You can start by saying you miss me too."

I remove the phone from my ear, press End, put it on silent, and put my headphones back in.

But I can't hear the music. The only sound in my head is my mom's voice on repeat like a catchy pop song. Except this isn't a song I want to hear.

You sound good.

Are you busy?

What are you doing?

I really miss you.

I stuff my face in my pillow and scream till my ribs hurt. Then I stop and do it again.

You can start by saying you miss me too.

That was a joke, right? It had to be. I don't remember my mom having any sense of humor, but that right there is Dave Chappelle–level comedy. Maybe that's why part of me feels like bursting out in a belly laugh. My eyes are closed so tight I can feel the pressure on my temples. I just spoke to my mother.

THE VOLUME ON MY HEADPHONES ISN'T LOUD
enough. I need to hear this music. I need to kill this other
voice that's trying hard to rent space in my head without
actually paying for anything. Staring at my iPad, I can see
that this illustration is turning out much better than I
expected. That color theory class is actually doing me some
good. Not just the one I'm taking now, but the one I took
when I was still in high school. My dad put me in graphic
design classes the year after he won full custody. I was
fourteen and remember being afraid to tell him that I
wanted to be a fashion designer. Not that my dad is scary
or anything; I just didn't want to risk seeing him fold his
lips together and stare down at me with those prophetic
eyes. It's not really his height that makes him intimidating
or that he can still easily throw me over his shoulder
without a grunt. It's those eyes. Behind those dark stares
are expectations. My dad imagined his way to where we
are now, and the silent expectation was that I would imagine something even greater for myself. But the odds of
making it as a fashion designer are probably worse than

making it to the NBA, so yeah, I wasn't jumping at the chance to break the news to him. And when I finally summoned enough courage to tell him, he wasn't jumping at the possibility either.

"You sure this is what you wanna do?" he asked. "Because it's okay not to be sure. You're barely a teenager, Coi. You should be trying a bunch of different things just to see what you like."

Maybe if I wasn't standing in front of him to see his eyes narrow, to feel his mind thinking ten, twenty, thirty years down the line and calculating the odds of me having a great life, I wouldn't have felt so anxious.

"Yeah . . . yeah, I think I'm sure."

My dad could've killed the idea right then. Told me that I was a kid and that I had no idea what I really wanted and shouldn't be closing the door on every other possible career to chase this dream that like one percent of one percent of people achieve.

"Okay, I'll make you a deal," he said. "If this is something you're sure about, then I'm with you. I'll do whatever I can to help you and buy whatever you need to get started. But there's one thing you have to do for me."

"What is it?"

"You have to learn how to do graphic design."

"Umm, okay. Why?"

My dad is a copywriter and a ghostwriter, a career that none of my friends understand even after I explain it.

"Trust me, if you learn graphic design, you'll always be able to make money. And you'll be able to put that money toward building your fashion career."

What he said didn't really mean much to me back then. I just wanted to do fashion, so I agreed. I got to take sewing classes on the weekends and my dad put me in graphic design classes twice a week. Now I'm eighteen years old, in my first year of college, and already getting paid to design magazines for indie publications and build websites for startup businesses. I guess sometimes parents actually know what they're talking about.

As grateful as I am for the money I'm making, fashion is still the vision. My Instagram is like an ode to the nineties, which is the decade I was really meant to be raised in. I've watched *Catwalk,* like, ten times — Kate Moss and Naomi Campbell might as well be gods on earth. My last post was about Aaliyah. Everything I wear is because of her, and with every piece I design, I'm thinking of one of her music videos or what the outfit would look like if she wore it on stage.

With all the sewing classes I took throughout high school and my obsession with watching every single YouTube video I could about fashion, I really didn't need any creative training. I'm taking fashion business in college so I can learn how to sell my clothing line. I'm trying to be one of the one percent of the one percent. I don't care how crazy those odds seem.

And this course is teaching me something. I'm learning how to market, learning about trends and finding a manufacturer and branding and shipping. So much of this stuff comes down to numbers.

Numbers.

One thousand six hundred and ninety-nine days. I know what that number means. That's why I hung up the phone.

It's hours after the call when I finally hear the front door of our apartment unlock and feel a wave of relief. Normally I just wait for my dad to knock on my bedroom door and tell me he's home. He always stands in my doorway for a few seconds to ask what I'm doing before heading into the bathroom or starting dinner. This time, I rush out of my room and meet him in the hallway while he's taking off his boots.

"My mom called me."

My dad chuckles like he thinks I'm not serious, but when he sees the look on my face he knows this is real.

"What? When?"

"A little while ago." I'm always looking up when talking to my dad. Even when his boots are off, he's still tall enough that I can see the bottom of his chin.

"Did you answer?"

"Yes."

"What did she say?"

I shrug my shoulders and follow my dad into the kitchen. He turns on the tap and uses the dish soap to wash his hands.

"She didn't say anything, really. I hung up on her."

We both burst out laughing. It's our favorite thing to do together. But I know my dad won't let me get away without giving him more info.

"So you hung up on her?"

"Yup."

"Why?"

This should be an easy answer. I can name at least a dozen reasons off the top of my head. My dad's leaning up against the sink waiting for me to say something. I'm searching through my mind thinking of which of those reasons is the most obvious. Which one makes me hate her the most?

The necklace?

My dad's still waiting. I'm still searching.

My sister?

Now my smile is gone.

One thousand six hundred and ninety-nine days?

I can't catch my breath. My dad's already pouring a glass of water from the fridge. I'm hunched over with my eyes closed, trying my best to focus on inhaling long and deep through my nose and exhaling through my mouth.

"Just breathe, Coi. You're okay. Just breathe."

My dad says this as he's rubbing my back. Tears are streaming down my face, faster with each memory. I'm trying to wipe them away as quickly as they're flowing.

I don't cry. Not for her. Not ever.

Tears are pooling under my chin. After another minute, my breathing slows down and my dad hands me the cup of water.

"That hasn't happened for a while," he says. He guides me to the couch, and we sit down side by side. I guess I should be grateful that this is the first panic attack in almost a year. They started the summer before high school, which is the same summer my dad won custody, which is the last summer I saw my mother.

I keep the cup in my hand so I have something to look at besides his face and can hide these teary eyes that make me look like some kind of victim. I can tell he's thinking through what to say. Actually, he probably knows exactly what he wants to say but is thinking through how to say it.

I'm his little girl. His only child. The reason for most of the drama in his life but hopefully most of the joy, too. Sometimes I forget that my dad's my dad. That this person I can talk to about all my firsts was the same age I am right now when he had me. Thinking about that freaks me out. There's no way I could take care of a baby right now. No way.

"What you gonna do?"

"I don't know."

There's something I have never told my dad, which I feel kinda bad about. But I did actually see my mom last summer.

It was weird. Me and my best friend, Jes, were hanging out at her house when my aunt texted me and asked if I could do her hair.

"Just a few braids," she said. She was almost nine months pregnant at the time so I felt like being nice, plus I really love my aunt. She's my mom's half-sister, but whatever half she got is the half I wish my mom had. She's also the only family member on my mom's side who's kept in touch with me since I've been with my dad. We mostly only text, but every once in a while, she'd invite me over and I'd feel brave enough to agree.

Me and Jes jumped in an Uber and when we pulled up to my aunt's townhouse, she was sitting on her porch.

"We might have a little problem," my aunt said as we made our way up the driveway. "Your mom just called and asked if she could drop your sister off. Of course, I didn't tell her you'd be here . . . how you wanna handle this? I can call you an Uber if you don't wanna stay."

Just the thought of seeing my mom made my stomach sink. I looked over at Jes.

"Don't look at me. I live with my mom. I see her every day."

I rolled my eyes and turned back to my aunt.

"Can I just wait inside? She's just dropping her off, right? So if you meet her outside, she won't have to come in."

"I can do that."

My mom lives only a few minutes away from my aunt so we hustled inside. I was still anxious, though. I thought about hiding in my aunt's bedroom closet just to be sure. I also thought about leaving altogether, but it was too late for that.

It couldn't have been two minutes later when I heard dance hall music blaring from outside. My mom clearly still knew how to make an entrance. Instead of retreating to my aunt's room, I tiptoed to the front window that overlooked the driveway and shifted the blinds just enough to get a peek. And there she was. My mother. Standing close enough for me to tell her whatever I wanted. She smiled with my lips, spoke with my voice, pointed her feet outward when she walked, the same way I do.

I had to fight the urge not to run outside. All the animosity was melting away faster than the chocolate ice cream Jes and I tried eating in the Uber. But I didn't move. Not one inch. I just stood there, at the corner of the window, looking at the person I feared and pitied and hated and never trusted, and watched her drive away.

I'm not sure why I never told my dad about that. It's almost like I've been processing it for all these months. And there was something special about that day; I got to see my sister. Kayla was like nine the last time I saw her, so seeing her four years later was like meeting a different person. When I first split from my mom and reached out to my aunt to speak to Kayla, she told me that talking to Kayla probably wasn't a good idea. That my mom was telling Kayla she didn't have a sister any more. That I wasn't part of their family. There was only one time Aunty let Kayla speak to me on the phone, and she said she spent the rest of the day reminding Kayla not to tell her mom because they'd both be out of the family, too.

When Kayla first came inside, I just sat on the couch, crossed my legs and pretended like I didn't see her. But as soon as she turned that corner, she came running over and jumped straight on top of me and wouldn't let go.

"You're crushing me."

"I don't care. You smell so good."

I could feel the breeze from the ceiling fan in the center of the living room. Watching the blades spin felt like being put in a time warp and my mind flashed through all the years of Kayla's life I'd missed. All the birthdays when I would've helped her put on her favorite outfit, all the times I would've combed her hair, how many times I would have shut my bedroom door because I was tired of her in my room.

Does she hate me?

That was the thought that snapped me back to the present. I never got to say goodbye to Kayla, and who knows what my mom told her. What she's been telling her.

Kayla never left my side the entire time I was braiding Aunty's hair. She stood most of the hour, passing me strips that I twisted into Aunty's curls, talking the whole time, articulating words like she read the dictionary for entertainment.

Where do you live?

What do you do for a living?

Do you still go to school?

How much money do you make? All easy questions to answer.

"Why did you leave?"

I knew that one was coming. One thing we both got from our mom is that we always say what's on our minds. We literally can't help it. I knew that question had been on Kayla's mind for years, and she finally had me right in front of her to ask it.

"I didn't leave. Not exactly."

"I don't get it. I remember hearing you and Mom arguing, which was, like, normal. Then you were just gone and Mom said you weren't coming back."

"I know that's what it looked like, but it wasn't like that." I thought about telling Kayla everything. Start to finish, all the stuff that happened before that day, but that would be cruel. As intelligent as she is, she wouldn't understand that she was collateral damage in a battle she probably didn't even realize was happening.

"Are you getting along with your mom?" I asked Kayla.

"She's your mom, too," Aunty snickered, and I tugged on one of her braids.

"You're right. Okay. Are both of you getting along?"

"Mom is Mom," Kayla said.

"What's that mean?"

"You didn't answer my question." I thought she'd forgotten

about that. "Why did you leave?" I stopped braiding Aunty's hair and turned to Kayla.

"I promise one day I'll tell you everything. One day, but not right now."

Now I look at my dad standing in front of me and think the same thing. I'm not ready to tell him everything. Not just yet.

———

I finally fall asleep to Snoh Aalegra in my headphones, but I wake up suddenly. I look at the time and it's only 3:33 a.m. Leaning over to look through my blinds, I can see that the sidewalks are damp from a light snow that's still falling. There's something about the street lights reflecting off the concrete surrounding the park that feels like a love story. Not the shitty rom-coms that my dad watches. I mean stories like *Love & Basketball* and *Jason's Lyric*. Old-school movies that I've become obsessed with.

I turn back over on my bed and instinctively grab my cell phone. Three missed calls, all from Aunty, all after midnight. I check my texts and she's messaged me, too.

Your mom got into a car accident. At the hospital. The one close to my house.

I sit up and read the messages over and over again. What does she mean *accident*? Hospital? Why would my mom be in the hospital?

As my brain is trying to compute, I'm already banging on my dad's bedroom door.

"Daddy!" I push it open and he jumps up.

"What? What's going on?"

"My mom got into a car accident. She's at the hospital."

My dad looks just as confused as I did when I first read Aunty's text.

"C'mon, Dad. We gotta go."

I throw sweats over my tights and hustle into a black hoodie my dad bought when we went to California a few summers ago and rush out the door, my dad pulling on a sweater right behind me. My jacket's still in my hand when we're waiting for the elevator.

"Did your aunt say anything else? Did she let you know how Crissy is doing?"

"No. Nothing. I've called her back a few times but she hasn't answered."

It's a thirty-minute Uber ride from downtown to the hospital. I'm staring out the window the whole time. The snowfall is picking up and the flakes look big enough to catch and hold in the palm of your hand.

Don't . . .

Don't . . .

Don't . . .

I'm doing everything I can not to think. When any thought comes into my mind, I force it back out. There's no point in thinking right now. No point in wondering about anything, assuming anything, feeling good or bad or whatever other emotion my body is trying to pull out of me. Every light I see through the car window is streaking. It's like a thousand candles flickering in the dark.

I feel the buzz from my phone on my thigh.

Emergency part. Room 225.

We pull up in front of the hospital and I don't open my door. Dad's already out. He bends down from his side of the car with the door still open.

"You coming?"

I don't answer. The door handle feels slick. The door itself feels heavier than it should. Walking through the hallways, I'm still shutting out thoughts. Not all thoughts, just those ones. The ones banging at my temple like a police officer with a warrant.

When we get to the area the nurse directed us to, I see familiar faces in the waiting room. Aunty is here. She spots me at the same time I notice her and comes hustling over to give me a hug. Kayla is right behind her. Both of them look like they haven't stopped crying since Aunty's been calling me.

"They don't know," Aunty says. "They said they don't know."

Her tears are out. She's still hugging me and I don't know what to do. But I see Grandma Lady and I think she's staring at me but she's actually staring past me. That's when I first notice that my dad isn't beside me anymore. He's a few feet away with both hands in his pocket, looking down at the floor.

I realize how awkward this must be for him. These faces are all familiar to him, too, but as friendly as bitter exes. I never thought of this part when I was waking Dad to come to the hospital with me. He hasn't seen or spoken to anyone from my mom's side of the family for just as long as me, the difference being that I share the responsibility of blood, a responsibility that's turned into a burden, I'm sure. But there's no allegiance to my dad, not from anyone here.

Grandma still hasn't moved. She's sitting in a full pink tracksuit with her winter jacket on the chair beside her. Her expression is hiding her thoughts, which is partly how she got the nickname Lady. Apparently, even at five and six years old, she sat with her back straight at the dinner table, knife in one hand, fork in the other, cutting her food into pieces and placing it in her mouth without making any mess. Now today, even with her daughter lying on a hospital bed, her back is still straight.

"None of us seen her yet," Aunty says. She's rocking her son, Pharaoh, side to side in both of her arms. He's sound asleep and looks so much bigger than he does in the pictures Aunty sends me. "These doctors aren't telling us nothing. Only that she's alive but in critical condition."

"What happened?" I asked. "Did she crash into another car?"

"No, another car crashed into her. She was getting off the highway close to home when it happened. The guy wasn't drunk or nothing, they say, just speeding through the red light."

I've been in the backseat so many times when we've crossed that intersection. It's easy for me to see my mom turning on her indicator to make the left. She was always so careful with her girls in the car. To think, another two blocks and she would've been home. Or maybe if she'd waited one more second before she made the left, she wouldn't be here.

"Baby Coi." I turn around to see Dave standing with a tray of coffees in one hand and a Starbucks bag in the other. It doesn't matter how many years have passed, I'll always recognize Dave's voice. He sounds like Westside Gunn from Griselda, who I've been listening to on repeat for the last year.

Dave rests the coffee and bag on an empty chair and gives me a hug. He's my mom's fiancé, or husband now, I think. At least that's what Aunty told me. Doesn't matter, though. He's Kayla's father and that's enough for me.

Of all the messed-up things my mom has ever done, he's not one of them. So even though the scar curving down the left side of his face is what made him attractive to my mother, remnants of his days running block to block, he's as sturdy as the CN Tower. Been that way since he came into our lives, when I was about four. It's been a while, but I doubt anything has shifted dramatically enough for me to feel any different.

"You're a full grown-up now," he says.

"Not yet, but I'm getting there."

"Why is he here?" Dave motions his head to my dad and I know my dad can hear what Dave just said.

Dave doesn't wait for me to answer. He approaches my dad and asks him directly, "What are you doing here?"

My dad keeps both hands in his pockets but is looking Dave straight in his face.

"My daughter's mother is in the hospital. Do I need another reason?"

"Here comes Mister Smart Guy. '*My daughter's mother.*' You mean your baby mother? Or baby mother isn't part of that smart guy vocabulary of yours?"

"Dave! Stop." He and my dad are nose-to-nose like two boxers the day before a big fight. Dad isn't saying anything. Dave looks like he still has a lot to say.

"You take Coi away from her mother for years and now you think you have a right to be here." The less agitated my dad looks the more animated Dave gets. "Crissy wouldn't

19

want you here. No matter what the situation. So why don't you do us all a favor and . . ."

"Dave!" I say again. "This is my dad. He needs to be here with me. And you need to chill out."

"He's right." Lady's words are like a fireball from one of those *Game of Thrones* ships. "Crissy wouldn't want him here. I don't want him here. It doesn't really matter what anyone else thinks."

Lady is still sitting down with her back as straight as a wall.

"Coi will be fine," Lady says to my dad. "You're not the only one here who knows how to raise kids."

My dad looks at me and shakes his head.

"I'm out," he says.

"No, we're out."

I grab onto my dad's arm and we hustle through the hallway like there's a flame chasing behind us. I peek back at my grandmother to see her arms folded. She's still watching our every step as we pass through the double doors that lead out of the waiting area.

"You shouldn't have done that." My dad says this as soon as we're out of sight. "You should be here with your mom."

"I know. But I wasn't gonna let them talk to you like that. They don't even know what they're talking about."

"Doesn't matter. I'm the outsider here. At least in their eyes."

Dad is probably right. He usually is.

"Honestly, part of me feels like I shouldn't be here either," I say. "When Aunty told me I couldn't see my mom, I was almost relieved. I don't know if I'm ready for all this."

I know what my dad is going to say before he says it.

"The universe knows best."

Of course it does. And clearly my dad doesn't know what else to say. It's the same explanation he gave when we moved into our apartment after months of searching. It's the same explanation he gave when he finally got full custody of me right before I graduated middle school. It's also what he says when the Raptors win, so not really sure what to make of that.

———

The Uber ride back home doesn't feel as grueling. It's still dark outside. Small piles of snow along the sides of the road are like flares guiding us the entire way. I think about calling Jes. I know she'd answer even though it's too early for life right now. Calling Derrick is not even an option. We've been going out for like four months and I really like him, but he's going to think he has to come rescue me and that's not what I need. I'm not exactly sure what I need right now, but it's not that.

We get there much more quickly than I expected and both Dad and I head straight to our rooms. It's like we instinctively know there's a battle ahead and want to make sure we get enough rest to endure.

Tomorrow's already here and we'll need all the energy we can muster. For now, my head's on the pillow and my eyes are glued to the ceiling. My last thought is of my mom lying in the same position.

The universe knows best.

STILL NO CHANGE THE NEXT DAY. THE DOCTOR SAID she hasn't opened her eyes since they wheeled her into the ER. She still can't breathe on her own. They use words like "severe" and "life-threatening" when talking about her injuries.

Every time one of those words comes out of their mouth, I can feel my grandmother watching me. She's in the same pink tracksuit, so I know she's been here all night. I can tell she's brushed a bit of foundation on her face, but no matter how stoic she keeps her expression, her eyes give everything away. She's just as hysterical as Aunty was when she texted me the news. She's just as scared as Dave is that he will lose the mother of his only child. I know repression when I see it. I'm a repression master.

My dad stayed home today. We both agreed that would be best. He was really only there to support me, but I'm a big girl now. Plus I know my mom's family; they won't let up. It'll be a fight every day for my dad so staying home is the right move. And the truth of it is that he and my mom didn't have any kind of relationship for a long time. They've been feuding since I could speak in full sentences. I don't know a

22

world where my mom and dad got along. Strange, but I can probably say the same thing about me and her.

My dad's done all he can to create a nice little bubble for us, and inside that bubble is just me and him. Anyone else we let in needs permission and also needs to follow the unspoken rules that they promise not to disturb the bubble and that they will leave the bubble the way they found it.

My dad's greatest fear is that someone will pierce through this thing. All it takes is one tiny hole to suck all the air out of his creation. My mom's phone call was a dull blade that our bubble was strong enough to keep out. Her being in the hospital is a machete.

Sounds dramatic but I swear that's what it feels like. And when I get back to the hospital late this morning, I'm wearing all of that drama on my face.

"You okay?" Aunty is reading my mind. We're sitting side by side in the waiting area sipping chai Dave bought for us from this café at least six or seven blocks away. They've both been here all night, too, and with the size of the bags under their eyes, I'm not even sure they slept.

"Yeah, I'm good." I wonder if she thinks I really mean that. Because I do. I feel okay. But maybe that's why she's asking me. I guess I should be crying. I should be breaking down in my grandmother's arms begging the doctors to keep my mother alive. The fact that I'm leaning casually back on the chair scrolling through missed messages on my phone is probably causing my aunt to worry.

"She loves you. You know that, right?" I kept my head straight and didn't say anything. "She does. She talks about you all the . . ."

"You don't have to do this, Aunty."

"Do what?"

"Make up stories about who my mom is."

"I'm not making this up. She loves you, Coi. I mean that."

"Did she love me for the last four and a half years? Did she love me when she walked me out of her house and handed me to Dad?"

Aunty and I are far enough away from Dave and my grandmother that they can't hear what we're saying. Kayla isn't here. Aunty said she's with Dave's side of the family.

"I'm not saying she was perfect."

"She didn't have to be perfect."

The doctor interrupted our conversation just as I was about to get up and walk away. Lady and Dave walk over to where we're sitting to hear what she has to say.

"Crissy is still in bad shape, but she's stabilizing. We'll let you see her, but only one at a time for now."

"Is she awake?" Dave asks.

"No, she's still in a coma. We're not exactly sure when she'll be awake or if she'll be awake. But right now, you should go see her. One by one, please."

The doctor walks away and we all just stand there. Dave is shaking his head. Lady looks for a seat and sits down. I'm already thinking of a way out of this.

"You should go first, Mom," Aunty says. "It's whoever after that."

We're all sitting together now. Lady has been in there for close to half an hour and I'm secretly thankful. The longer she stays, the longer before I have to go in. I'm crossing my fingers that the doctor will change her mind by the time it's

24

my turn. She'll come out here and say that my mom has had enough or that they need to move her to another room that we're not allowed to visit.

Aunty goes in next. She's in and out in five minutes before Dave goes in.

"You'll be fine," Aunty says. She puts her hand on my knee that's been shaking since Lady went inside. I nod my head and keep my fingers crossed.

Four years seven months and twenty-five days.

It's been that long since my mom has looked me in the face. That long since she's made me tea in the morning with way too much sweet milk. Since she told me to keep still while she braided my hair so tight, tears dripped out the corners of my eyes. How many times did she tell me to take the bus to school because she was too tired to drop me off?

That didn't bother me as much as it probably should have. By the time I was nine, I was taking the bus to school almost every day. At first it was a little scary, but I got over it quickly because when my mom dropped me to school, she'd be blasting nineties reggae music so loud that everyone always turned to look at us. I'd much rather be scared than embarrassed.

At least that's what I thought back then. Right now, fear is eating away at me from the inside. It's bringing up memories I haven't thought about in years. It's making me think of ways I could get up and leave and never come back and just deal with the fact that I don't belong to this family. Not anymore.

My knee still hasn't stopped shaking. Dave slowly walks by me and sits down without saying a word. I should get up now. I should walk down the hallway and into that room.

"I don't wanna do this." I feel everyone's head turn toward me. "This was a bad idea. I'm not ready for this."

"Coi." Aunty drags out my name like it isn't just three letters.

"No, seriously. The doctor says my mom isn't even conscious. What difference does it make if I go see her or not?"

"Your mom might not be conscious, but you are. And you need to do this for yourself, not her."

"Leave her," Lady says to Aunty, with just enough patois to remind you she means business. She hasn't said anything to me directly since I got here this morning. "You can't force her to care. If Coi don't want to see her mother, that's her problem."

"You think I don't care?"

My grandmother crosses her arms and her legs. "I know you don't care," she says, still not looking at me. "You let your father brainwash you into thinking that your mother is some kind of monster when everything she did was for you."

"Brainwash? Are you being serious right now? Aren't you the same one who kicked my mom out of your house when she was sixteen? Was she an angel or a monster when you didn't even come to the hospital when I was born?"

"Stop!" Dave's voice sends us back to our corners. "Stop it. All of you. My kid's mother is in there fighting for her life and you guys are out here arguing about bullshit."

Dave is standing up now, and with everyone else seated next to each other, it's like he's literally talking down to us.

"Coi, if you don't wanna go in there, don't go. But I'm telling you right now, you'd be making a big mistake."

Dave walks away but not before giving me one last glare.

26

I look over at my aunt and she nods her head. Without saying another word, I turn off my thoughts, stand up and head straight for my mom's room.

This hallway feels like the green mile right now, except I'm not walking to my own death. Actually, I hope I'm not walking to anyone's death, but that's the thought that kept my leg shaking and why I didn't want to be walking down this hallway in the first place.

Outside of my mom's room, I can peek in through the glass and see her face. Two long braids are dangling over her jaw but not enough to hide the swelling and bruises. It looks like most of her other braids have been cut. I cover my mouth to stop myself from screaming and crouch to the floor.

Long deep breaths.

Long deep breaths.

I wish my dad was here. This is too much. I need to stop trying to convince myself that I can handle this. Maybe I really can't. I can walk back to the waiting area right now and tell everyone that I sat with my mom. They wouldn't know the difference. I should do it. Just walk away. Walk away before this panic attack goes full blast and I'm the one lying down in one of these rooms.

Long deep breaths, Coi. Stand your ass up.

As soon as I catch my breath, I push open the door and step inside. I take a few more inhales and get closer. Close enough to shift the two braids away from my mom's chin so I can see her whole face. Even through the swelling I can see the person who made me. The same person who pushed me away.

My own braids are wrapped loosely in a top bun. There's a metal chair with a green seat beside the bed, but I'd rather stand. There's way too much going on inside me right now to sit down. Too much I'd want to say. Too much I'd let myself think about. And I don't want to think right now because there won't be anything that will make me feel better about standing here. And the only thing that should matter right now is my mother fighting for her life.

Even that thought feels false. Fights are supposed to be violent. They're supposed to be loud and aggressive, all adjectives that describe my mother perfectly. Maybe that thought isn't false, after all. If anyone is used to fighting, it's the person lying in this bed with a sheet covering half of her body.

"Can you hear me?" I whisper those words like we're not the only ones in the room. "Can you really hear me?"

The beeps from the heart monitor sound like warnings. Like when those big dump trucks are reversing and don't want anyone or anything in their way. My mom is that dump truck, except she doesn't send out any warning when she's ready to go off.

The first time she called me a bitch I was only four years old. We were at the McDonald's drive-through and she ordered me nuggets and fries but I wanted ice cream, too.

"Don't be a greedy bitch. Take what you get and be happy."

I was so young, I couldn't even talk back. I'm not even sure I knew what bitch meant, so it wouldn't have mattered anyway. It was still just one of those words I'd heard repeated in the living room when my mom had her friends over.

Why am I even thinking about this right now? That's why I didn't want to come here. Why I don't want to sit down. I don't feel what Aunty feels when she looks at my mom. My heart doesn't move like Dave's does when he and my mom are together. The only thing that moves is my mind and it's moving backward. Back to the past, our past, my mother and me and that past is what led to close to five years of separation.

That's about all I can take. I turn and run out of the room, press my back against the wall in the hallway and slide to the floor.

Deep.

Breaths.

"Are you okay?" A nurse crouches beside me and puts her hand on my shoulder.

"Water," I say in between breaths. "Water, please."

The nurse disappears and comes back within a few seconds with two coned cups that are barely more than a sip each. I guzzle both and keep breathing.

"Is that your mom in there?" I nod my head. The nurse sits beside me with her legs straight out and that's when I first realize how tall she is. She looks at me the way a parent is supposed to look at their child when they're not feeling well.

"Memories," she says. "No matter what, no one can take those away."

The nurse rubs my shoulder, lifts herself off the floor and walks away. My breathing is totally calm now. A small burst of energy gets me to my feet and suddenly I'm feeling pretty good. When I get back to the waiting room, Aunty is pacing around like she's been waiting for me. Lady is trying her best to listen in on our convo without turning to face me.

"You okay?" she asks.

"I think so. I'm gonna take off, though. I'll be back tomorrow."

My dad isn't home when I get in. I head straight for the tub to fix a hot bath.

Sitting in the tub, I can feel the anxiety slowly drip away with each drop of water that trickles off my skin. The bathroom door is closed, so I can't hear the trains passing or any bells from the streetcars.

I stay in the tub till my skin starts to prune. When I finally get to bed, I'm already drifting off.

Memories, I think to myself. Life is all about memories.

THE HAND THAT'S GUIDING ME THROUGH THE DOOR feels familiar. She's looking straight ahead, so I can't make out her face, but I know I know her. When we get inside the room, two nurses and a doctor are standing over a pregnant woman instructing her to push. The sound of the screams stops me from taking another step.

"Keep breathing, Crissy. You're almost there. Keep breathing and give me another push."

"Crissy?" I whisper. I take another step forward and narrow my eyes. "Mom?"

Her eyes are closed and the veins on her neck look like tree branches. That's when I notice that standing beside my mom, with just as much sweat on his forehead, is my dad. He's holding one of her hands in both of his but isn't saying anything. His jeans look four sizes too big and his red T-shirt is nearly down to his knees.

"Good job, Crissy. One more push. One more big push."

My mom takes three or four deep breaths, gives one big thrust, and out comes a baby. I step in even closer, close enough that I could touch the baby's toes if I wanted to.

"Is that . . . me?" The newborn is bloody and icky but it's definitely me, screaming at the top of my lungs while the nurse sprays me down with what I guess is water. My dad is grinning and my mom hasn't taken her eyes off me. When they put me on her chest my arms are still flailing, but I'm quiet. The entire room is quiet. My mom is whispering something to baby me but I'm not close enough to hear it.

I jerk awake on top of my blanket and scan my room. Every part of my dream is rushing back to me and I replay it over and over again. I've never remembered a dream in this much detail, where I could make out people's voices and actually smell the strange mix of blood and something unrecognizable in that hospital room.

Even sitting on the corner of my bed, I can still see the wrinkle in my mom's forehead as she's pushing one last time. And I can see myself. Like really, I just saw my birth. I was right there.

"Coi, breakfast. You hungry?" My dad's standing outside my bedroom door with his head poking in. "It's banana pancakes and I only put cinnamon in the ones that I'm eating."

"Umm, yeah, sure. I'll be out there in a sec."

"You alright? Need some water?"

"I'm fine. Go away. I'll be out in a minute."

By the time I get to the living room, Dad's halfway through his pancakes. The honey's already beside my plate and so is a glass of cranberry juice.

"Eat. It's getting cold."

My dad looks almost the exact same as he did in my

dream. A little bit more facial hair, but that's really about the only change.

"What were you wearing when I was born?"

"Huh?"

"When I was born, what were you wearing? Do you remember?"

"Umm, I think I was wearing . . ."

"A red T-shirt down to your knees and really baggy blue jeans?"

My dad puts his fork down and looks at me like I just read his palm.

"Yeah. Yeah, I'm pretty sure that's it. I used to have a picture of it somewhere. How did you know that?"

"I don't know. I probably saw it in one of your mom's photo albums or something. When's she getting back?"

"Who knows. She's in Trinidad for months at a time now that she's retired. What made you think about your birth, though?"

"Not sure," I lie. "But now I'm absolutely sure that I didn't get my fashion sense from you."

Dad laughs and fakes like he's about to throw a piece of pancake at me.

"I saw my mom yesterday. Like I saw her, saw her. She was just lying on that hospital bed not moving."

I wait for my dad to respond but he doesn't say anything.

"I touched her face. It felt . . . normal. Like I thought she would feel different but she felt so normal. Then I tried talking to her but didn't know what to say so I ran out. Like literally ran out of the room and sat on the floor outside the door like an idiot. I don't know what's wrong with me."

My dad is chewing slowly, listening to what I'm saying, but the way he's looking through me I know he's calculating all the different ways he can respond.

"Nothing's wrong with you," he finally says. "There's no right way to deal with this. There's only what you feel."

"But that's the thing, Dad, I don't know what I feel. Like, I should be sad, right? Like devastated kinda sad. But when I was in that room, all I thought about were all the reasons me and her haven't talked in years. That can't be normal behavior. Something's definitely wrong with me."

These pancakes are too cold to eat anymore. Plus I'm not really hungry. That dream is still on my mind and the fact that I saw my birth is a bit disturbing. Or really disturbing.

"When are you heading back to the hospital?"

That's another disturbing thought. I don't want to be at the hospital every day waiting for some kind of catastrophe. Even though the building is filled with doctors and nurses and all types of medical specialists, there's this absence of hope that looms over me when I'm there.

"I'm putting together some logo options for a client plus I have a class later, but I'll probably stop by after that."

Dad nods his head and gets up from the couch.

"So I guess you're not helping me move any of this stuff into storage?"

"You got this. I'll help move it into our new place, how about that?"

"How about you get out of here?"

TRYING TO FIGURE OUT WHICH COLOR FABRIC TO choose in this patchwork class for a design I sketched out a few days ago feels pretty pointless when my mom's lying in the hospital, but I get through it. I get through all of my classes without a hitch. The entire time, I'm waiting to get hit with an overwhelming wave of grief — an agony so heavy I have to run out of my classroom and down the hallways as professors and students wonder what the heck is happening.

But despite the images of clear tubes and swollen lips that remain with me the entire day, I muster enough creative energy to put together color pallets. I find enough social energy to nibble through a beet salad at lunch with Jes and Derrick.

"You sure you good, girl?" It's the second time Jes has asked me since we sat down. I don't know why I haven't told her yet. I'm not about to tell her now, with Derrick here, but she should've known already. Jes is beyond a best friend; she might as well be my twin. Neither of us like pop music, we both never had a serious boyfriend until we started college, and both of us think that some babies are ugly. Jes is the friend I bring to the cottage that me and my dad rent every year for my birthday near the end of summer.

"Happiness depends upon ourselves." I don't know why I just said that. It's an Aristotle quote that we read in class sometime last week. We've been reading a lot about happiness and all these strange theories that supposedly intellectual people come up with.

"Deep," Jes says sarcastically. "But for real, you're good, right? Because if you're not . . ."

"I'm good, Jes. For real."

I wish Derrick wasn't here. I hate saying that because he's actually not a moron like most of these college boys and he really does like me, but whatever's inside me needs somewhere to escape, and with him here, it feels trapped.

"Coi's always okay." Derrick is watching me as he says this. We've been together long enough for him to catch the signs when I'm not myself. "Tell her, babe. You can handle anything by yourself, right?"

I know Derrick isn't being serious but I can tell that Jes is getting annoyed. It's not that she doesn't like Derrick; she just doesn't like anyone trying to get at me. But Derrick is a teddy bear. We met on campus during orientation but didn't actually talk till our second or third week. The dean wanted a mural painted near the entrance and me and a couple of art students raised our hands to do it. We organized times between our classes every day for two weeks, paintbrushes and paint cans on top of layers of newspaper, designing and coloring in images we sketched out in art books before getting to the real thing.

"This is really cool." Derrick was off to the side staring at the half-done mural. He didn't say it to any of us in particular, so when none of us answered, he took a more direct approach. He stepped on top of the newspaper and got close enough to the wall that we all gasped at the same time.

"I think the tip of her hair should be red," he said.

"I think you need to back up, buddy," I responded, "before we start tossing paint all over those Air Forces."

"Oh, so you do talk?"

"Yeah, I do, and I just told you what's about to happen if you don't get away from that wall and let us get back to doing our thing."

Derrick backed away with both hands up.

"Okay, okay, relax. I thought you were coy, but that's not you at all."

I rolled my eyes even though I thought it was funny. Plus I'd be lying if I didn't admit I was impressed he remembered my name. Derrick winked and walked away but we didn't talk for like another week, when we finally finished the mural.

"You guys did a good job," he said.

"Thanks, but we're not guys."

"I know, I just meant . . ."

"I know what you meant." When we talk about this conversation today, he always says I was being mean. I thought I was being playful.

"You just won't give me a break."

Maybe I was a little mean, but he was annoying. Cute, but still annoying. I let him walk me to the streetcar that day and the day after that. We were always with groups of my friends when we walked and I would feel Jes hawk-eyeing Derrick the entire way. I love that girl.

Picking at these beets with a fork Jes packs in her knapsack, I'm trying my best to keep up with what she and Derrick are talking about. But I need to head to the library to finish up some work before my next class.

Finally finished my last class and now I'm standing at the bottom of the staircase leading outside typing the hospital address into Uber. I stop myself right before pressing Confirm.

"Coi." I mouth this to myself quietly as the rest of the group files past me into the already dark early evening. "This is not optional, Coi. You need to go to the hospital."

My thumb still hasn't moved. My knapsack is way too heavy and now I can't decide on whether I should go back to the hospital or just head home. I can already hear my grandmother talking shit about how I don't care and that I'm a terrible daughter and blah, blah, blah. Who cares what she has to say? My mom's been on her own since she was sixteen. Sixteen! Whose fault was that?

Where was Lady when my mom got expelled from school for the first time? I know where. She was home packing up my mom's shit so she didn't have to deal with her anymore. My mom told me it was eight months before my grandmother finally sucked up her ego and came to visit me. Eight whole months. I was already walking by then. Actually, she came the day after I took my first steps. My mom sent her a long text about how she was missing her granddaughter's life and how she would regret not being part of it. Apparently, my grandmother didn't even reply. She just showed up the

38

next day like nothing happened. This is what West Indian mothers count as an apology.

She's the last one who should be ridiculing me for anything, but she will, and so will Dave. He'll be a lot nicer about it but he'll still have something to say. The scar on the left side of his face isn't just a reminder of why my mom was attracted to him, it's also a reminder that Dave wasn't always a real estate agent. But he started changing his life around even before I left, and now, with the flexibility of his schedule, he can make a few calls, arrange some showings, and be back and forth from the hospital without it really impacting his life. And because I'm in college and freelancing, he'll expect the same from me.

But none of them understand. How can they? Maybe Dave a little bit because he was there. He saw some of what was happening, but he wasn't me. He didn't have to endure it. He didn't have to endure a mother telling him that the sound of his voice made her sick. He didn't have to put up with being called a bad sister because he stayed in his room most of the day to avoid the chaos outside those walls.

I knew. When my mom walked me out to my dad with garbage bags full of clothes and told me that my last name wasn't hers so I didn't belong in her house, I knew it was the last time I'd see her. Even with the fight for full custody, Dad thought my mom would still be part of our lives. When a year passed without so much as a text, he finally got the picture. And now this happens. This accident. Now all of a sudden I'm supposed to care again.

Are you home?

I text that to my dad and he replies that he is.

Meet me at Union? I'm starving.

He's already at a table near the back, away from the windows, when I get there.

"Tea, Dad? Really? You couldn't get us a bottle of wine?"

"Did you turn nineteen when I wasn't looking?"

"Whatever. You know every time we go out, waitresses think I'm your girlfriend and offer me the wine list without ever asking for ID. You really should be flattered."

The waitress pops up on cue and asks what I'd like to drink. I tell her a glass of sauvignon blanc and she compliments my choice.

"I ordered some oysters, too," Dad says. "And some soup. I had a feeling we might be here a while."

I still can't believe he's my father sometimes. He definitely helped raise me but it also feels like we grew up together. I told him the other day that I have to be the only child in the family who's experienced nearly every level of economic status. The super-broke stage when he was washing cars for a car rental company at the same time he made twenty bucks a night in tips selling lottery at the bingo hall. He couldn't even afford to buy me birthday gifts back then. I was five when I realized we didn't have much money, and from that point on I'd only ask for small things like books and pencil crayons.

Then he started making some money and we moved into the Liberty Village apartment we live in right now. Private art classes, a family trip to California; life started feeling pretty good. Now he's buying his first house. Not a house, exactly, but a townhouse. It won't be ready for a couple more months but we're moving into his mom's house next month so we don't have to keep paying rent while we wait. She'll still be in Trinidad like she usually is, so I'll still get my own room. Our new place has three bedrooms and Dad says I can use the den to do my fashion stuff. He says we're upper middle class now. I say we're hood rich.

"Why didn't you go visit your mom today?"

That's the question, isn't it? Why, why, why?

"I don't know. I'm trynna figure that out, too." A full bowl of oysters comes out and I dive right in. "Right now I feel like I'm making a mistake. Like I should be there. I should've been there all day with everyone else."

"But . . ."

"But I don't know. That's what I'm trying to tell you. I really don't know what to feel or think or do."

My dad hasn't touched any of the oysters and I'm already slurping up my third.

"Do you remember the last time you spoke to your mom? Before all of this happened. Do you remember her walking you out to my car?"

"Yeah."

"Do you remember the first thing you said to me when you got in the car?"

"Yes, I said that's the last time I'll ever see my mom again."

"Yup, but when she called the other day, you still answered your phone, right? And you still woke me up in the middle of the night to rush to the hospital as soon as you heard what had happened, right?"

"Okay, what's your point?"

"My point, my rude daughter, is that there's a part of you that still instinctively cares for your mother and that's okay.

It's okay to feel that way just like it's okay to feel conflicted about those emotions. Visiting her at the hospital while she's fighting for her life isn't you making a decision on your relationship, it's you being human."

"So I should go see her?"

"Yes, you should."

"Why didn't you just say that?"

"I just did."

In my room after Daddy/Daughter dinner, I text Aunty for an update and to tell her that I'll be there in the morning. No change, she says, which makes me exhale audibly into my pillow. Cuddled up in a fetal position with my blanket up under my neck and my head tie wrapped extra tight, I can't shake the thought of my mom lying in the same position. Not seeing her today is firing up my imagination, but everything I visualize is steering me to a bad place. My therapist says thoughts are thoughts and real life is real life, so I know this is just my subconscious trying to negotiate whatever reality I'm struggling to deal with. But that doesn't mean I'm not fighting to keep my eyes open right now because I'm scared of what I'll see once I slip away.

"Hey." My dad is standing in my bedroom doorway. He usually waits till I tell him he can come in, but he walks to the edge of the bed without an invitation and sits down cautiously. "You know, Coi. Your mom . . . your mom did some bad things to you."

"That's an understatement."

"I know. It is. And I know it's been you and me against the world for so long. But . . ."

"But what? There is no 'but' after that, Dad. If there was a 'but,' you wouldn't have fought so hard for me to be with you."

"You're right, but I'm just thinking of your mom in the hospital right now and I don't want something to happen that makes you feel . . ."

"Makes me feel what?" I'm up from under my blanket now. I'm sitting cross-legged in the middle of my bed forgetting that I was ready to pass out just a few moments ago. "Let me tell you a story." He's going to love this one. "I was about twelve and Kayla was about seven or eight years old. Don't ask me why, but my mom was really mad at Kayla. So mad that she walked to the kitchen and grabbed the broom. Kayla was already in the living room crying and when she saw my mom come back with the broom, she begged her. She freaking begged her."

"Coi, you don't have to do this. I know how bad your mom could get."

"No, I want you to listen. Everyone thinks they know but you don't. Kayla begged her not to hit her with the broom. I was sitting on the couch when Kayla ran to me and grabbed onto my arm. I could feel her whole body shivering like someone left her out in the cold. Do you know what my mom did? With her seven-year-old daughter begging her not to, do you know what my mom did?"

I can feel myself shiver as I tell this story, and realize that my window is open like it always is before I go to sleep, that February breeze cold on my shoulder and toes.

"She lifted up that broom and brought it down on the side of Kayla's leg. Kayla was screaming, Dad. Screaming."

"She hit Kayla with the broom?"

"Yeah. Yeah, she did. Then she tried to do it again and I jumped up and grabbed the broom. I tried to wrestle it away from her but she pushed me to the ground." I've replayed this story in my head so many times but have never vocalized it to anyone. Ever. The way my dad is looking at me right now, he probably wishes that was still the case.

"Can you imagine what it feels like to be hit with a broom over and over and over again? On my arms, my legs, my back, my ribs. I was curled up on the floor trying to deflect the blows and crying for my mom to stop at the same time."

"Coi." I can feel my breathing picking up and I'm trying to catch my breath before it gets worse. My dad reaches out his arm and lets me fall into his lap while I'm inhaling and exhaling as slowly as I can manage. "I'm sorry you had to go through all of that. And no, I can't imagine what that must've been like."

"I think the only thing that made her stop is that I stopped trying to block her from hitting me. She didn't even say anything. She just tossed the broom on the floor and walked off with me lying on the floor barely moving. This was my mother. This is my mother."

It's another hour before my dad leaves my room. I don't tell him any more stories about my mom. That one was more than enough. I know Dad had a different agenda when he walked in here, but after the broom story, we just sat for a while, quietly. Eventually, we found a way to laugh. We always find a way.

DARKNESS.

Like the kind of dark that only happens in bedrooms at the cottage where the glint of city lights don't filter past your windows.

It's just me in a room I can feel is present despite the lack of light. The darkness is the only way I know that I'm dreaming, so in that way it's like a guide. A guide I follow with careful steps, one foot in front of the other, one foot in front of the other, slowly, until I feel like I'm in the middle of the room. Then I sit down, cross my legs, and wait.

The first glow of light lifts the darkness from underneath. When the room is bright enough for my eyes to make out objects, the only thing I see is my mother seated in front of me.

"Do you miss me?" My first instinct is to laugh. Her legs are spread open like she's just finished a yoga workout, and she's leaning back on both hands. She knows the answer.

"What's going on here?" I say. "Are you haunting me?"

"I'd have to be dead to be haunting you and I'm not dead yet."

"Yet?"

"I shouldn't say that. I don't know if I'm gonna die, but I'm still alive in real life. You would've known that if you went to visit me today."

I'm still not convinced that this is happening. That my mother is sitting close enough for me to reach my hand out and have her take it. I should be pinching myself frantically. Screaming and hollering and jumping around so that I can wake up and forget this dream like the thousands of others that have disappeared into my subconscious once I opened my eyes.

"Who are you?" I say this without a smile or smirk on my face.

"Who do I look like?"

"I know who you look like but who are you? And why is this happening? Why are we here, in this dream, together, and talking to each other?"

"You and your father must be closer than ever by now. You used to cry so hard every time he left the apartment. It got so bad that we started putting you in the bathroom so you wouldn't see him leave."

"What are you even talking about right now? What does it matter how close me and my dad are? That has nothing to do with you anymore. Or actually, it has everything to do with you."

"I always felt it. You know that, right? How close you two were. I always knew."

Of course she knew; I wasn't trying to hide it. And what choice did I have? Seriously. It was either love the parent who abused me or love the one who didn't. My dad would get so mad to hear me oversimplify our bond like that, but it doesn't change the fact that it's true.

"You know what story I just finished telling my dad?"

My mom looks at me like she already knows the answer but doesn't want me to say it out loud.

"I told him about the time you smacked my sister with the broom before I tried to stop you. Then you turned on me and started beating me while I was on the floor. You remember that? The good old days, right?"

"I remember."

"Of course you remember. You better fucking remember. *You* did that. You! And when I tried fighting back you swung that broom even harder."

"I do remember, Coi. It was the first time you fought back. It was also the first time I really looked at myself in the mirror."

I can feel the heat building on my forehead, which is strange because I'm not supposed to feel anything in a dream. But it's like it doesn't matter what world I'm in; my mother still doesn't get it.

"You? You looked at *yourself* in the mirror?" I'm laughing so loud I hear echoes from all sides of whatever room or space this is. "Whatever you saw must've been fucking evil because that wasn't the last time you hit me. Not even close."

My mother's not as sharp with her tongue in this world. She's just sitting there, no steam coming out the top of her head, no cutting me off before I get a chance to explain myself, no switch to patois, which is when I know there's no coming back, no working out the problem. In this world, she's just sitting there. I unfold my legs and raise my knees to my chest.

"You just left me on the floor. My whole body was bruised. My ribs could've been broken. You didn't even bring me to the hospital. I don't get it." I'm fighting to keep my voice even. "Why would you do that to me?"

I don't know if I've ever asked my mom why in real life. Actually, I know I haven't. The reason never mattered to me. I just wanted it to stop. I wanted her to stop. I was gone long before my mother let me go.

"Walk with me, Coi." My mother stands up and offers her hand. I look around the space for some kind of clue about what's happening. A sign of what I should do or when this dream will end.

"I can stand up on my own, thank you."

The figure pulls her hand away, turns around and walks away confidently in a direction that doesn't seem to lead anywhere.

"Where are you taking me?"

"Wrong question, my daughter. The real question is where do you want to go?"

Before my mom finishes her sentence, three elevators appear. They're numbered but otherwise identical, and I can see both of our reflections in the steel doors that are all closed.

"Choose one," she says.

"Are you granting me wishes?"

"No, Coi. What I'm trying to do is get you to choose an elevator. I won't have to explain anything else after that."

I'm pinching my forearm while stepping closer to the middle door.

"This one." The elevator doors pull away from each other to open. "Let's see where this takes us."

Both of us step inside the elevator and it ascends without a sound. It's a full minute before it stops and the doors open again. When I step out, I'm in a familiar space, one I recognize instantly.

The walls in my old bedroom are distinguishable only because of their bareness. They're painted some kind of off-white with no accent colors, no holes from thumbtacks poked through posters or other mementos, only bareness.

"The walls are a giveaway, right?" my mom says.

"They sure are. You said we weren't allowed to cover them with anything and that if you came home and saw even a scratch, well, you know the rest."

"You're right. I did say that. And plenty of other things, too."

Who is this agreeable person standing beside me? Because it's not my mom. Not the way I know her to be. Not the one who cursed me out and wouldn't let me leave my room for two full days because I ate a veal sandwich when I was staying with my dad. I didn't understand why I had to follow her dietary rules outside of her home, especially when the rules didn't make any sense.

We can eat steak and beef but not veal.

No pork except bacon.

Seafood is fine but no sushi.

When my dad dropped me off and I still had half a veal sandwich left over from lunch, she grabbed me by my collar and pulled me up the stairs. Not long after, I heard her blasting Daddy for buying it, but I'm sure he didn't even know veal was a problem. He probably hung up the phone more confused than anything.

49

"You didn't let me dream," I say. "It's like you hated me for wanting to be someone other than you."

"I never hated you, Coi."

"Doesn't matter. That's what I thought, it's what I felt, so you hating me was very real in my world."

My mom opens her mouth to say something else, but nothing comes out. Instead, she walks back to the elevator and motions for me to follow. As the elevator rockets upward again, my mom closes her eyes.

"I never hated you, Coi. I don't ever want you to think that anything I ever did wasn't out of love."

"So that broomstick is how you showed affection?"

Her eyes are still closed, her head tilted like the answer is somewhere beyond her. The elevator stops.

MY EYES OPEN CAREFULLY. I'M TOUCHING MY FACE with both palms, widening my eyes to scan the sketches and photos and affirmations that cover my bedroom walls. As my gaze is shifting, I remember the lift of the elevator, the darkness that I navigated, my mother. I spoke to my mother.

All of the images from my conversation come rushing back. I see the curve in my mom's chin when she asked if I missed her, I see my room as bare as it was when I left it, I see me, the me I am now, speaking words to my mother in a world that couldn't be real. But it all felt just as real as me lying under this blanket.

Is she alive? Is that what this is about? That thought gets me in and out of the shower and out the door without breakfast. Instead of going to the waiting area, I head straight for my mother's room and peek at her from outside the door. She's still there. A nurse is also in there with her, changing the IV drip.

The relief I feel seeing my mom lie motionless but with life still inside of her is the most emotional I've felt since Aunty texted me about the accident. I back away from the door, but the thought of walking over to the waiting room to endure stares from my grandmother makes me want to call an Uber and head back home.

But that's not the deal I made with myself. I'm here for my mom, not them. And Aunty's probably here, so I'll have someone to talk to who doesn't treat me like I'm the white girl from *Get Out*. Plus I hope her son, Pharaoh, is here again. I can squeeze those cheeks all day. Still, I feel like being alone right now, so grabbing a cup of peppermint tea and wandering the hospital halls sounds like a better plan than being around anyone.

The hallways in hospitals are so wide. I can stay to one side and not be in anyone's way, so that's exactly what I do. I'm almost pressed against the walls as I stroll past patients in wheelchairs, families looking for their loved ones, and triage nurses registering more patients who may or may not be sick. I've always thought that going to the hospital is like deep-sea diving in the darkest parts of the ocean; you just never know what you're going to find. And that uncertainty either leads people here or prevents them from taking the plunge.

I'm on a different floor now. Not exactly sure which one but these hallways feel different. Fewer people are walking around, except for two little girls who must be twins. My guess is maybe five or six, both with their snow pants still on with the straps snug on their shoulders. One is chasing the other around a group of rooted chairs while a woman, who I'm assuming is their mother, sits and turns the pages of a book she's halfway through.

The sound of the twins giggling as they move in circles is the only sound I can hear. When is the last time I laughed like that? I mean just like that. Not because something was funny, but because I was so captured by a moment that nothing else mattered. Just whatever was feeding my soul. And whatever was feeding my soul felt so good that all I could do was laugh.

The vibration from my phone brings me back to the sterile floors and dull walls.

Are you coming? It's a text from Kayla. I guess it's time I join the crew. I let Kayla know that I'm already inside the hospital and will be at the waiting room in a minute. The twins have settled on their mother's lap. She holds them both under her arms, moves their hair aside and kisses their foreheads. They don't notice I'm there.

"DINNER'S READY."

It's hard not to laugh every time Derrick's mom, Lucy, yells that out loud. You'd think she spent hours in the kitchen mixing sauces and sautéing delicacies. Dinner tonight is from a new Middle Eastern restaurant that Lucy tried a few weeks ago and hasn't been able to stop talking about.

We're in the kitchen with boxes of food spread across the island. Me and Lucy are sitting beside each other and Derrick is facing us.

"You are absolutely going to love this, Coi. It's the most delicious thing I've tasted in years."

"Okay, Mom. Just like that seafood we ate like a week ago."

"I can't help it that I find the best restaurants. You should be thanking me." Derrick shakes his head. "Can you believe him, Coi? I know you like all the food we eat, don't you?"

"I do."

"She has to say that. She's being nice."

"I don't say things just to be nice. You should know that by now."

I still remember the first time I came to this house. I thought I had the wrong address. It was early in the fall and his front door looked like those paintings of Roman temples. The front foyer alone was bigger than the apartment Dad and I were living in. We hung out in his study, no Jes there for protection, and watched season-old fashion shows and *Open Door* from *Architectural Digest* on YouTube.

His mom came home with dinner in hand — spring rolls, red curry shrimp with white rice and pad thai — and invited me to stay.

"There's more than enough," she said. "And Derrick doesn't usually bring friends over, so you're more than welcome."

When I went to shake her hand, she pulled me close to her white blouse and air-kissed me on both cheeks.

"You can call me Lucy."

"I'm Coi," I said.

"Coi. What a lovely name."

Lucy's hair was up in a loose bun and she smelled like the Chanel perfume she would end up giving me months later. Her heels made us the same height and she had a hint of color, but not the kind you get when you tan.

Those evenings became routine, including his mom sitting with us telling horror stories about tenants.

Sitting next to Lucy on the island now, seeing how she and Derrick interact, makes me want to tell them both what's happened to my mother. Every time I rip a piece of flatbread, I feel the words rising up from my stomach but getting stuck right before I open my mouth. The other part of me feels like I shouldn't even be here. That I should be spending every minute I can at the hospital. When I left there today to come to dinner, I almost rerouted the Uber to go back. But then I got all in my head about answering questions from Lady and decided to come.

"I think I might stay at the condo this weekend, Derrick. Will you be okay for a couple of days?"

"I think I'll survive."

"What condo?" I ask.

"I haven't told you about Mom's hideout spot?"

"Oh, stop it, son. I'm not hiding out. I'm recuperating." Lucy lifts her head and closes her eyes like she's meditating.

"Mom has this condo downtown that she goes to whenever she wants to get away from me."

"Don't listen to him, Coi. First of all, it's off Lake Shore near Windermere, so just outside of downtown. Second, it's the first place I bought with my own money when I started doing real estate. We only lived in it for a couple months and Derrick was too young to remember that, but I've kept it all these years because it means a lot more to me than a sale. Now I just go there when I want to unwind. Or sometimes I let friends who visit me from out of town stay there."

"That's so cool. You should show it to me one day."

"I would love that." Lucy takes a sip of wine, then stands up. "As a matter of fact, I can show you some pictures right now. Let me grab my phone."

Lucy leaves the room and comes back with her cell phone in hand. She scrolls through images of a fully furnished, two-bedroom apartment that overlooks the lake. The balcony is furnished like a backyard and the leather couches look like they've never been sat on.

"Wow," I say. "This is really beautiful, Lucy. I can't wait to see it in real life."

"I'll take you there whenever you're ready. As a matter of fact, you can stay there sometimes, too."

Derrick looks at his mom like he doesn't recognize her.

"Seriously? You'd let me stay there?"

"Of course I would. I know you and Derrick have only been seeing each other for a few months, but you're stuck with us. And even if you two don't work out, you're stuck with me."

Lucy gives me a soft hug and I squeeze her tight. Tighter than I should be for such a light moment. I should be letting go but I can't pull my arms away.

"Hey, you okay, honey?"

No! I'm not okay. My mom is dying. I shouldn't be here. I should be in Aunty's arms crying.

"Yeah . . . sorry." I'm finally able to peel myself away. "I'm fine. Just . . . I've had a rough couple days, I guess. But I'm okay. For real. I am. Sorry."

Lucy pulls me in one more time and kisses my cheek.

"There's nothing to be sorry about, Coi. You are family. Plus, Derrick has seen me cry plenty of times. He's used to it."

That lightens the mood enough for us to get back to finishing our dinner. Later that night, Derrick and I watch a movie while Lucy is asleep in her room.

"You gonna tell me what's up with you?"

"It's nothing, D. I just had a moment. I'm good." He knows I'm lying. He also knows that badgering me won't do any good.

"Okay," he says. "Whenever you're ready, let me know." He interlocks our fingers and turns back to the TV.

"WE'RE GOING TO SEE IF CRISSY CAN BREATHE ON her own today," the doctor announces. Aunty stands right next to the doctor with Pharaoh in her arms. "We think there's a good chance she will be strong enough to do it, but there are no guarantees."

When is there ever a guarantee? It's been four full days since my mom's been in here and uncertainty has been the only constant.

"When are you gonna do this?" Dave asks.

"We're getting her prepped right now. We'll be able to let you know how it went within the hour."

This is the part I can't deal with. The waiting. Most of the time, we're sitting or standing, pacing or eating, waiting for the doctor to validate our faith or fracture our hope. Even when I'm at school, it feels like I'm waiting. Waiting for class to end. Waiting for the Uber to pick me up. Checking my phone every other minute I'm not at the hospital, hoping not to see any urgent messages. This has been the routine for the past few days, and as much as I trust and respect doctors, I hate that we're forced to put my mom's fate in the hands of humans rather than whoever we're praying to.

The anxiety of this wait is so heavy that my grandmother leaves the waiting room. She does it without any announcement and we all just watch her go.

"I don't know how she's holding her shit together," Dave says.

"You think she's holding it together?" I say. "She's a fucking wreck. Just because she's not curled up on the floor in tears doesn't mean she's okay."

"She's a strong woman, Coi. Give her some credit."

"And you're a man so you don't even get how messed up it is that you're saying that right now."

Aunty nudges me with her elbow but I can see a little smirk on her face. Even though my timing may be inappropriate, I know she's secretly high-fiving me for what I just said. She's the one who made me watch Chimamanda Ngozi Adichie interviews when I was just eleven years old. She made me read *The Handmaid's Tale* when I was twelve and then sat me down for an hour after I finished reading it to discuss some of the themes.

"You're going to love yourself," she would say. "No matter what else is happening around you, make sure that you love yourself and love being a woman. We have secret powers and you can only access them when you know who you are."

Might be a lot for a preteen, but it was exactly what I needed. Between my mom and dad fighting all the time and the crazy stuff that went down at my mom's house, it could've been easy for me to fall into a trap of self-loathing. And I was there, or at least I was heading there. But Aunty wouldn't let that happen.

She lived with my mom for a few months when I was like five or six, but even when she moved out, she was always present. I've spent almost as much time with her as I have with either of my parents. Maybe it's because I was her first niece. Maybe it's because she knew my mom was fucked up and wanted to protect me. Whatever the reason, I'm grateful.

We all look up when we see the doctor approaching. Before she's close enough to say a word, I'm analyzing her face for any kind of clue. She's usually holding some kind of mobile device or clipboard in her hand. She's not this time. Is that a good thing? Bad thing? Anything?

"I wish I had better news, but Crissy isn't able to breathe on her own yet. This doesn't mean it won't happen, but we need to give her more time."

My grandmother isn't back yet. She's the first person I think about when the doctor gives us the news. Pharaoh starts crying like he somehow understands what's happening. Aunty doesn't even try hushing him. She finds the edge of a chair and is staring at the ground in disbelief. Kayla doesn't hold back her emotions.

"So, umm, what do we do now?" Dave asks.

"We wait," the doctor responds. "It will be at least a week before we try again, probably longer."

Dave nods his head and I avoid his eyes. I avoid everyone's eyes. The doctor walks off, and when she's far enough away I chase after her.

"Wait. Doctor. Just one sec."

"Hi, you're one of her daughters, right?"

"Yes. That's my mom you just told us about. I just . . . I mean, does she really have a chance? I know you're not

60

supposed to assume anything or whatever, but I just wanna know. Does she have a chance?"

Her face is too kind to belong to a doctor. There's too much hope in her eyes for all of the tragedy that I'm sure she's witnessed.

"Can you remind me of your name again?"

"Coi."

"Oh yes, how could I forget such an interesting name? Well, Coi, your mother does have a chance, and we're doing everything we can to keep her alive. It's likely that nothing much will change over the next few days, so this might be a good time to get some rest."

Those kind eyes are reassuring. She touches my arm before walking away again and it adds another drop to whatever evaporating hope I have left. I look back to see Dave trying to comfort Kayla. How is Aunty dealing with this?

"What did the doctor say?" My grandmother pops up in front of me with her purse over her shoulder and a bottle of water in her hand.

"Where were you?" I ask.

"Never mind where I was. What did the doctor say?"

"That my mom can't breathe on her own yet and they have to wait at least another week before they try again."

Lady keeps her head high and doesn't take her eyes off me.

"And how do you feel about that?" she asks.

"What do you mean how do I feel? Did you hear what I just said?"

I don't know where this conversation is going but I'm already thinking of a way out of it. Lady's looking me up and down and I just know she's revving up.

"Tell me something, Coi. If your mother wasn't in the hospital, would you ever see her again?"

Aren't grandparents supposed to be loving? Aren't they the ones who spoil you with attention and let you stay up later than your parents allow? Don't they give you money for your birthday and tell you stories of how their own kids drove them crazy? Lady's been around for most of my life but was never really available. Not for me. I see so much of my mom in her, and I always have, which is why as soon as I was conscious enough to make decisions, I decided to keep my distance.

That distance grew until my mom routinely had to threaten me to make me call my grandmother. Or she'd call me downstairs when she and Lady were on the phone and put it on speaker. I'd put on my best "good little grand-daughter" voice and tell Lady how much I missed her and that she should come visit soon.

"I don't know, Lady. But why does that matter right now? I'm here. We're all here for my mom. I don't really think this should be about me."

"Oh really? So now you want to think about someone other than yourself? Where was that humility for the last four years?"

"Do you really wanna do this now? Because I don't, and I'm not going to. And I think you need to get your facts straight because I didn't abandon my mother, she abandoned me. Oh, and it's been almost five years." *Get the numbers right, Lady.*

"You sound ridiculous. A mother would never abandon her child."

"Really? Because I thought you left my mom on her own for years."

I'm doing everything I can not to grab this woman by the throat and squeeze until she can't open that maroon-lipsticked mouth of hers. I shouldn't even be talking to her. Like really, why am I even giving in to this?

"What are you two ladies chatting about over here?" Dave is a lifesaver. I don't have much willpower left in me, so thank God he came over.

"Nothing," I say. "I was just about to leave. I'll be back tomorrow."

Lady still hasn't moved. I'm already on my way to give Aunty and Pharaoh a hug and kiss Kayla on the cheek. I just want to get out of here and get something to eat.

I message Jes and tell her to meet me at Mildred's, a café we go to on weekends for French toast. When I get there, Jes texts me that she'll be a few minutes late. I use the time to call my dad and let him know what the doctors said about my mom.

"And how are you dealing with this, Coi? Maybe this is a good time to talk to your therapist. What do you think?"

"Maybe. I'll send her a message later and see if she's free."

"But how are you feeling right now? Are you still at the hospital?"

"No, I'm having brunch with Jes. Just waiting for her to get here."

I'm having brunch with Jes.

Hearing those words come out of my mouth makes me nauseous. What am I doing here? Seriously. My heart suddenly feels as frigid as the walk from the GO station to the café. It's like someone injected my veins with ice and nothing I do can get me to the right emotional temperature to thaw it out. By my dad's silence on the phone, I can tell he's thinking the same thing. He's been my emotional caretaker for so long. He knows when I'm fighting against something; he knows when I'm holding so much inside that I'm ready to burst. But right now, he's trying to calculate and he can't make me make sense.

"I'm okay, Dad. Really. I just don't know why I'm okay."

I can picture Dad's concerned face. He's probably biting the inside of his cheek and looking off to the side like his words are somewhere in the air and he just has to find them.

"Come home when you're done. I'll make you a banana and Nutella smoothie."

"With a little bit of honey?"

"Yes, honey."

If we're not the corniest father/daughter combo, I don't know who is.

By the time Jes shows up, my jacket and scarf are off and I'm halfway through a cup of black coffee. The waiter brings over the menus but we let her know that we're here for the French toast.

"I still don't get why you drink coffee. And then you don't even put anything in it. Yuck. It's like you're a fifty-year-old white man. Like one of my dad's friends or something."

Jes is just as unfiltered as I am, except she does it with a smile and a straightening of her glasses. When I first told her that me and Derrick were a thing, she asked me for his number. When I asked her why, she said she just wanted to make sure that Derrick had no excuses. That she wanted to give him fair warning that if he ever did anything bad to me, she'd do terrible things to him. I'd thought she was joking, but when I asked Derrick if he'd spoken to Jes, all he said was that my friend was crazy.

"I need this coffee right now. It's been a rough morning, or a rough few days, really."

"Tell me."

I take another sip and spill everything. From my aunt messaging me when my mom first got into the accident, to the drama with my dad and everyone else, to the strange dreams I've been having.

"Stand up," Jes says. She shuffles out of her seat and is already standing over me. "C'mon. Up you go."

When I'm up, Jes gives me a big, mamma hug and presses my head into her shoulder.

"Do we have to do this in here? In front of everyone?"

"Yes, we do, Coi. And you know if you don't give me a real hug, I'm not gonna let you go."

Jes isn't lying. She really will keep me standing like this, so I give in and go full embrace. It's kind of weird at first, knowing everyone's probably watching, but Jes is patting my back and petting the top of my head. When she shifts one of my braids, I feel my eyes tearing up. I duck my head further into Jes's shoulder and now I'm all-out crying. I'm sure people are looking at me like I'm crazy, like both of us are, but I can't see anyone and I don't care.

My sobs sound like a breakup on one of those rom-coms my dad watches.

"It's okay," Jes says over and over again, and it's like every time she says it I dive deeper into whatever state this is. Finally, I break away, and suggest we go back to my place.

When we get there, I realize how sparse it looks, with all the packing for our big move. But we still have our couches and beds here so that's all we really need. Dad sticks to his word and makes me and Jes banana and Nutella smoothies.

"I'm guessing Coi told you about her mom?" We're all spread out on the couch with our smoothies in hand.

"Yes, she actually just told me right before we got here."

"Sounds about right," Dad says. "At least she told you. You know how Coi gets sometimes."

"I know. We had a moment in the café, though. She knows I'm here for her."

"You two know I'm right here, right?"

Jes edges closer to me and lays her head down on my lap.

"Did she tell you about her dreams?" Jes asks.

"She told me about one dream. Have you had more, Coi?"

Sometimes Jes and I are a little too much alike. She says whatever she wants in front of whoever is there, including my dad. I didn't tell my dad about my other dream because I'm still processing it. Telling him about seeing my birth was strange enough, but this last dream was next level.

"I had one more the other night. It was really weird. I saw my mom or someone who looked and talked like my mom. I don't know; I'm still figuring that out. It's like I was reliving a moment, a bad moment, and then I kinda ended up in this dark space and my mom popped up in the room and we had a conversation."

"A conversation?" Dad asks.

"About why she thought hitting me and my sister with a broom was okay."

"Like that story you told me the other day?"

66

"Yeah, that same story. And that's another thing; she knew I didn't go see her at the hospital that day. It was so weird. Like, is she watching me? I don't know . . . it's like my mind is trying to cope or something."

Jes is up and in the fridge, grabbing a box of water.

"Boxed water," she says. "Someone finally gets it."

Dad ignores Jes and is clearly thinking through his next question.

"You should control it," Jes says. When I ask her what she means, she points to her temple. "I mean control your dreams. You're lucid dreaming, which basically means you're super aware that you're in a dream and can actually control how things go. So next time, take charge. You show your mom what you want her to see instead of letting her control things."

"Is that possible?" I ask.

"I think so. I've read about it but never done it before. You should try it and let us know if it actually works."

Control it? I was hoping not to have any of those dreams again. None of this is normal and I don't want it to be. I want this to be over and to go back to forgetting my dreams as soon as I wake up. The thought of seeing my mother again, of speaking to her in some *Inception*-type dream world, isn't something I'm looking forward to.

The only time I remembered my dreams was even more messed up than this. It was a few months after Dad got full custody, just after I turned fourteen at the end of that summer. I hadn't spoken to my mom at all, but I also hadn't seen or spoken to my sister, either. Then, for like three days straight, I had these wild dreams where I killed her. I killed Kayla.

I wasn't myself in those dreams. I mean, I was me, but me in the body of an eagle or some other large bird. And in each of those dreams, my sister was on the ground running away through the woods. I'd be hovering above her waiting for a chance to swoop down, and when I finally caught up, she'd be inside our mom's house and I'd scoop her up with both claws, lift her up through the roof and into the sky, then drop her thousands of feet down onto the concrete.

After my third night of having that dream, I told my dad and he did what any concerned parent with a premium insurance plan would do; he put me in therapy. Yeah, four-teen years old and already traumatized. I actually hated it for the first month, but at the end of our fourth session, my therapist told me that I didn't need to come back.

"Therapy is a choice," she said. We were sitting on single couches across from each other in the basement of her home. Half of the basement was set up like an office, with a black rolling chair tucked under a mahogany-colored desk covered with brown files. Bookshelves lined most of the walls and each shelf was filled to the edge with mostly hardcover titles. The other section of the basement had a small bar with two high chairs and about a dozen bottles of alcohol. A wine rack as tall as the ceiling occupied the rest of the wall. She's never once offered me a drink.

"This is about healing, and if I'm not the right person to help you get there, I'm fine with that. But it's important you get there, so maybe seeing someone else will make that journey easier."

I don't know if that was psychologist reverse psychology, but it worked. There was no way I wanted a different therapist, so I started giving in. Just a little at first. Longer answers, more eye contact. Then I started talking about random things like staying home from school to do my sister's hair because my mom was taking her out that afternoon. Or dropping Kayla off to school when she started kindergarten because my mom didn't want to wake up that morning. Or my favorite memory: opening my bedroom window so I could hear all the kids playing outside the complex when my mom wouldn't let me go outside for the whole first month of the summer.

Therapy has been helping me through all of this, and even though I still go whenever it feels like I need a tune-up, I don't know if there's any kind of therapy to tell me how to control my dreams where I'm speaking to my mother who's in the hospital. Dad hasn't said anything and Jes is not going to let up until I say I'll try, so that's what I say.

"But it's not gonna work. I don't even know what I'm doing."

"Sounds a bit wonky to me," Dad says. "But why not try it? Maybe taking control will make the dreams stop."

"I don't know how that makes sense, Dad, but sure, I'll try."

DAD IS FINALLY OFF TO HIS BOOK CLUB WHILE JES and I are still slurping our smoothies and scrolling through our phones.

"I sold out!"

"Sold out?" Jes asks.

I give her my phone, which is showing the sales on my website.

"Yeah, sold out. Remember that drop I did a couple weeks ago? It was mostly hoodies with a couple full sweat suits."

"Oh yeah, I saw that on IG. You sold everything?"

"Everything."

Jes grabs both my hands and flings them in the air with hers.

"Coi Douglas, fashion extraordinaire."

"Calm down. It was only twelve pieces."

"Yeah, and all twelve of them are gone. You're pretty much an icon now." Jes pretends she's walking down a runway, like designers do after their show, then stops and blows a kiss to me like I'm part of the audience. "So when's the next collection coming out?"

After me and Jes finish our smoothies, I get a text from Derrick asking what I'm up to. I tell him he should come over, and while we wait for him to show up, Jes is fireballing ideas on what my next drop should look like. Just before Derrick arrives, Jes also tells me that I should catch him up with what's going on with my mom. She says there shouldn't be any secrets between friends, especially since Derrick is more than a friend now. I'd been starting to think I'd never tell him, but I take her advice and let it all out, down to the doctors trying to get her to breathe on her own.

Now we're sitting at separate ends of the couch and Jes is sitting on the floor in between us. It's barely midevening, but outside is so dark that it feels closer to midnight. My dad's still out so it's just us, TV off with Derrick's Spotify playlist coming through the speaker.

He keeps looking over at me with these puppy dog eyes, which is making me regret telling him about my mom. I really hope he doesn't start asking me if I'm okay every other day. That'll put him on the fast track to a breakup.

"Wait, just one more question," Derrick says. Jes looks over at me to gauge my annoyance level, then lets him finish. "If your mom lives . . ."

"Really, Derrick?" Jes jumps in. "If?"

"My bad. When your mom gets better, will you talk to her again?"

I stop myself from blurting out "no" even though that's my first reaction. The truth is that I haven't really thought much about that. I don't want my mom to die. That I know.

"I don't know," I say. "And I don't really wanna think about that now. I hope she gets better and she's normal or

71

whatever. Like no crazy long-term health problems, know what I mean? But besides that, I don't know."

"I think you'll talk to her again." Jes says this like she can already see the future.

"Yeah? How can you be so sure?"

"Because we're the same people and I know your heart. You'll talk to her. Watch."

I shrug my shoulders and let Jes pat me on the knee.

"'K, one more question. Promise."

"Derrick!" Jes doesn't need to look at me this time. "You're going too far, bro. You're turning this into a therapy session."

"I know, I know, but you guys know all this stuff already. I'm just finding out. Of course I'm gonna ask a million questions. Just one more. I swear."

"It's cool," I say. "Let him get all his questions out now." Derrick smiles like a kid with a new video game.

"Okay, so you told me that it's been a long time since you've seen your mom. But when I ask you about the last time you saw her, you always say she walked you out of your house. I don't get it. Do you mean she walked out on you?"

It's so easy for me to go back there. I don't need a dream. The images of that day are just as vivid with my eyes open.

I'm already back in my old room. My mom is raging through my closet, ripping clothes from their hangers and tossing them on the floor.

Take it. I can hear her voice like she's standing right in front of me. *Take all of it.*

I can see the two piles of clothes from my closet on the floor. They're half her height but she's not done. She stomps over to my dresser and starts pulling out the drawers.

72

You don't wanna be part of this family? Fine. Take this. And this. And all of this.

"Hey," Jes says, and I notice her and Derrick staring at me, waiting for me to answer Derrick's question. "We don't need to talk about this. Seriously."

"I'm good. It's just . . . I can still see her. I can still see myself. I was in grade eight, wearing my red and black school uniform. Go Hawks, right? And my knapsack is on my back and I'm just watching her destroy my room and throw all my clothes on the floor. It's like it's happening all over again right now."

Jes and Derrick are quiet now. It's like storytime in first grade and I'm Miss Duncan, telling the most personal story possible.

"And everything's on the floor except for the dress she bought for my graduation. It was this dark pink, full-length gown that looked more like a bridesmaid kinda thing than something I'd wear to graduation, but she wasn't gonna let me have it. She brought it to her room and then came back with three garbage bags in her hand, still screaming at me."

"What was she saying?" Derrick asks.

"That I'm not part of her family. That I don't have her last name or her man's and Kayla's last name so I shouldn't be in her house."

I see myself picking up a handful of underwear and tossing them into a garbage bag. A handful of socks and tossing them into a garbage bag. Jeans, sweaters, the tank top I'd planned on giving Kayla. The tears on my face were already crusted from what happened at the school parking lot, before we even got to my mom's house. I can see her standing over

73

me, though, arms crossed, blurting out whatever she thinks will hurt me the most.

"Then she checks her phone and tells me my dad is outside waiting. I didn't even know she called him or whatever. I still didn't really know what was happening. She just told me to hurry up and pack my stuff and we were out the door."

Jes is looking at me like it's the first time she's heard this story. Derrick wants to know more.

"Where was Kayla?" Derrick asks. "Was she watching this happen?"

"I don't know where she was. When my mom told me that my dad was outside, I was just trynna get out as fast as possible. But she followed me downstairs from my room. She watched me put my sneakers on and then walked outside with me. When I looked back at the house, Kayla was at the window peeking through the side of the curtain. And she was only like eight or nine or whatever, but she's watching me and I'm looking at her and I can tell she doesn't really know what's going on. She doesn't know that's the last time she'll see me in that house. And I wanna wave. I wanna wave and tell her not to worry and that she'll be alright. But my mom just kept talking and talking."

"'Don't bother looking back.'" My mom's voice again, clear as the lake in Kincardine. "'You hate this house and love your dad so much. This is what you want, isn't it? You don't wanna be here anymore, right?'

"That killed whatever motivation I had to at least tell Kayla bye. And all of this was happening and I still didn't say anything back to my mom. Nothing. Not a word. When we get closer to my dad's car, my mom tells me that I'll never see my sister again. That's the last thing she said to me."

But she didn't just walk away. She watched me throw the three garbage bags in the back of the car. She watched me open the front door and lower into my seat. She watched my dad reverse all the way to the end of the complex, past the staircase, past where all the kids my age would be playing, and didn't move. I always wonder why she did that. If even for a minute, for a second, she changed her mind and wanted me back in her home. I remember, in the moment, wishing that she would chase my dad's car and tell me she was sorry and had made a horrible mistake and that of course she loves me and wants me close to her. That she wants me at all.

"That was day one," I say. "You know the rest."

My phone is on the floor, vibrating like a small drill.

"It's your Aunty," Jes says and passes me the phone. Before I can put the phone to my ears, I hear Aunty wailing.

"She's gone, Coi. Crissy is gone."

I'M NOT GOING.

My eyes are half open from another night of not being closed. I'm lying on my side thinking about reaching for that cup of water on my nightstand, thinking about turning over and mummifying myself in these blankets, thinking about shutting my eyes tight so I can see. But that's just it, I don't want to see anything.

"Hey." My dad's voice is gentle and the nudge on my shoulder even gentler. It's like time has reversed and I'm in my crib again, except my dad won't be lifting me up. No one will. "You gotta get ready. This is not something we can be late to."

Late? How can we be late to something that's already happened? My mom is gone. She's been gone for the five days I haven't slept. A funeral doesn't change that and so I don't move at my dad's urging. I don't respond to anything he's saying even though it's already noon and the funeral starts at 1:30. He's doing up the last two buttons on a dark blue dress shirt I've never seen him wear, his mouth forming words that are supposed to move me.

How do I tell him?

"If you hurry we can still have time to grab something quick to eat before we head to the church."

Last time I was in church was grade ten. Me and Jes were sitting at the back, more chatty than usual. Our teacher turned around a couple times to shush us, but she might as well have been talking to herself.

"Why are we even here?" I whispered to Jes.

"No idea. Let's get out of here."

"Now?"

"Yeah, why not? We don't believe in any of this stuff so why are we sitting here listening to it?"

I wasn't sure how serious Jes was till she got up and started excusing herself toward the aisle. Of course I got up and followed her right out while our teacher and everyone else bent their necks to see what the heck we were doing. When we got outside, we laughed all the way to the pizza spot and laughed some more while we filled our mouths with cheese slices.

There's no laughing today, though. Jes and Derrick will probably be here soon. I'm sure if I looked at my phone I'd have more than a few missed messages.

How do I tell them?

"I made some tea, Coi. You should at least drink something in case we don't have time to . . ."

"I'm not going."

The words almost burn coming out of my mouth. I can't see the look on my dad's face right now because the glass of water on my nightstand still has me in a trance.

"I don't understand. What do you mean you're not going?"

My eyes feel dim, like someone lowered the brightness on my phone. Dad knows what I mean. "I'm not going" is pretty damn clear. He's just shocked I actually said it and can't believe I could be serious.

But I don't say anything else. I'm not even sure what I could say to change the tone of my dad's voice or help him make sense of what he just heard.

"Coi, I need you to get up and get ready and I need you to do it right now."

Poor Dad. Now his tone is getting stern. When I still don't respond, he moves into my line of sight and crouches so we're face-to-face.

"Coi, are you listening to me? I said you need to get up and get ready. This funeral is not optional. We're going."

Maybe I should yell back. Maybe I should tell him to get out of my room and leave me alone because no matter what he says, I'm not going to this funeral. Maybe. But I still don't say anything. My dad's glaring into my eyes and I'm off in another world, a world where there's no way I'm moving from this bed. My dad starts pacing the room with his hands on his hips.

"Okay, I know this is hard for you, Coi. It's hard for both of us. I get it. But trust me, you don't wanna do this. You're gonna regret this one day and I don't mean like ten years from now. You're gonna regret this today."

He's probably right, but I've lived with a lot worse than regret. Plus it really doesn't matter, anyways. Add it to the mountain of other stuff my therapist says I need to face. I'm sure I'll get to it one day.

"Coi, say something." He pauses, but I don't say anything. "We have to go, Coi. You know that. You know you can't miss this."

I close my eyes all the way now and find enough energy to sit up against my headboard. I'm still wrapped in my blanket and I can only imagine what my face looks like from days of insomnia. "The only thing I know is that I'm not going to the funeral. I don't care how bad it looks, I don't care what anyone thinks, I'm not going."

We haven't been here before, my dad and me. I've never defied him like this. The closest we came to a real dispute is when he took my phone away for three days. I was fifteen and stayed out with Jes till after eight on a weekday. My dad was calling and texting but I didn't answer. And it's not like I was purposely trying to ignore him, it's just that me and Jes were at the lake drinking vodka for the first time and I got sick. We got lucky that Jes's parents were out on a date night, and she let me sleep it off at her house. By the time I woke up, it was after ten. My dad freaked out.

"Can you at least tell me why? This is your mom, Coi. And I get it. I really do. This is weird for you. Maybe weird is the wrong word but it's hard for you because of the history. I get it. But don't make this mistake. You can still deal with your feelings but you need to come to this funeral."

"No, I don't."

I flop back onto my side. My dad's still looming but he isn't saying anything. There's nothing really left to say and I think he knows that now. I don't say anything either. My eyes are half closed again, although I'm not sure they were ever fully open. I hear the door to my room shut but no footsteps. Still no footsteps. I close my eyes.

May

"FAVORITE MISTAKE." "THIS AIN'T LOVE." I'M SKIPPING "Heartbreak Anniversary." One more song before I get to "Vanish." I've been sitting in this bath for over an hour. My phone is lying on a mini-sized wooden table that I bought only for this reason. Every note Giveon sings sinks me deeper, but when the last beat drops, I reach over and press Play again. Play again. Again.

It's easier to get lost now. My new bedroom has an ensuite and enough space for a desk that holds my sewing machine. The den was supposed to be my playroom, but my bedroom had more than enough space so my dad uses the den as his office. Now torn, cut, ripped and half-sewn fabrics are under every step I take in my room, with tubes of fabric paint pushed up against the back wall. A day can pass where I only open the door to fill my water bottle. Some days I wake up at five in the morning and jog the sidewalks in the dark. Another day can pass when I sit in my room all day with just headphones.

Play it again.

I've stopped counting days since that day. It's May now, and we've been in our new townhouse since the middle of

March. Last month, I somehow managed to write my finals, complete my last assignment, and crawl through the end of my first year of college. As difficult as it was to focus on schoolwork, I signed up for a summer merchandising course because I needed somewhere to go three days a week that wasn't my bedroom. Once that class is done, I know where I'll be going. I know what's next. For now, I keep those plans locked in my own mind, a mind that hasn't felt like my own since that day.

I dunk my head under the bathwater, hold my breath long enough for my chest to burn, and then haul myself out of the tub. As I get dressed, I can hear my dad typing on his laptop in the den. When I pop up I let out a heave that drowns out Giveon's melodies. "Favorite Mistake." "This Ain't Love." I give "Heartbreak Anniversary" a chance, then press Stop before he gets to the chorus.

I know part of my dad is still dealing with disappointment and frustration that I didn't go to the funeral, which meant that there was no way he could've gone. Him showing up without me would've unleashed a firestorm of questions and accusations he wasn't ready to deal with. Not showing up at all was just as bad, but at least he could pause notifications on the backlash and not have to endure the looks of disgust and confusion over me, my mother's eldest daughter, not being there to say a few words, to hold my sister's hand, to cry in Aunty's arms as they lowered my mother's casket into the ground.

My dad didn't speak to me for a full week after I ditched the funeral. Then, a few days after we finally moved into our townhome, he sat beside me on my bed.

"Do you like it?"

"I do." I saw him biting the inside of his cheek.

"Are you . . . okay?"

I'm not sure that was what he wanted to say, but when he didn't correct himself, I thought about the question. "Am I okay?" We obviously weren't talking about the house anymore, but how was I supposed to answer that? Am I okay about what? My mom being dead? Skipping her funeral? Because the answer would've been no, I'm not okay with any of it. But is that really what he wanted me to say at that moment? *No, Dad, I'm not okay.*

Scrambled eggs and turkey bacon for breakfast. I unplug the kettle right before it starts whistling and pour it into a waiting cup filled with peppermint.

"Good morning," I say to my dad. He turns his head enough for me to see him smile but doesn't say anything. When I grab my plate and head back to my room, he wheels his chair around.

"You have plans tonight?"

"Derrick's supposed to come over," I say, "but we're just watching a movie. Why?"

"And you have class today? What time is it over?"

"Monday, Wednesday, Thursday, Dad. Today's the late class so I'll be done by six o'clock. Same schedule since it started. Why you asking me this?"

He taps his chin like he's calculating something, then asks if he can pick me up when I'm done class.

"Umm, sure." My dad only picked me up from school one time all year, and that was after my first day of classes. We went to eat gyoza and drink soup at one of his favorite restaurants close to our old apartment. All that to say I have a feeling he's up to something. I should pressure him. He always caves when I press him to tell me something he wants to keep secret, but I'll just smile and keep nibbling on these eggs like I don't know he has something up his sleeve.

He's already waiting at the corner when I get to Lake Shore. A string of other cars are parked along the side of the road, engines on with the windows rolled up on a rainy, late-spring evening.

"My poor hair," I say, "No one said anything about it raining today. I didn't even bring an umbrella." My dad smiles and pulls out into traffic.

The rest of the drive is quiet. AM radio. Housing prices skyrocketing. Sexual abuse claims at a university, which makes me think that I'll need to walk around campus with some kind of sharp object next semester.

Before they move on to the next topic, my dad pulls up on a side street and puts the car in park.

"You know what house that is?"

The house looks like it was built before Lady was born. There's no garage, but a cement driveway leads to a chipped white front door.

"No. What house is it?"

"This is the house you came to when you were born. Me and your mom lived in the basement, if you could call it a basement."

"This is it, for real?"

"Yup. See that side door right there? We had our own entrance, but as soon as we stepped inside, there's this narrow-ass staircase with the ceiling so low that even your mom couldn't stand up straight."

I'm barely listening to what my dad is saying. My mind is already picturing me in a stroller, arms and legs wrapped tight in a white blanket and my head covered in a polka dot hat.

"Me and your mom were so broke that we had to take the bus to the hospital when her water broke. People were looking at us like we were crazy. The bus driver caught the play and let us ride for free. We sat right up front and I don't know if this really happened or if I'm making it up, but I swear he started speeding."

My window is down, so there's nothing disturbing my view. The rain trickles into the car, some landing on my face, but I don't care. This is it. This is the house.

"Let's go inside?" he says.

"For real? We can do that?"

"Why not? Let's go knock and see what happens."

My dad raises my window back up and turns off the car. He must've been expecting I'd want to. How could he not? When we knock on the front door, a boy a little younger than Kayla pokes his head through the curtain, then turns around and yells out that there's someone at the door. We can hear footsteps descending down a creaky staircase before a woman props open the door.

"You made it," she says to my dad. "And this must be what all the fuss is about."

"We did. I told you we would." My dad looks at me with that annoying grin. I knew he was up to something, but this is definitely not the something I expected.

The boy, who I'm assuming now is this woman's grandson, sneaks under her arm and shifts his eyes back and forth between my dad and me.

"Here's the key," she says. "I'll put some coffee on. You drink coffee, dear?"

"Yeah, I do. Thanks."

She smiles and looks at my dad. "Full grown, this one, eh? Bet it still freaks you out every time you look at her."

"Every time."

We stride over to the side door and my dad sticks the key in the lock.

"How long have you been planning this for?"

"Not long," he says, that grin still plastered on his face. "Or maybe too long. Who knows. Watch your head."

Dad wasn't kidding about this staircase. I have to limbo to get to the bottom before I can finally stand tall. "Looks the exact same," Dad says. "I think the fridge might be different, but everything else looks just like how I remember it."

Remembering this place wouldn't have been hard. It's one room with the only separation being the wood from the tile that marked the kitchen.

"We put your crib right there in the corner. We had a pullout bed right beside it and the TV was over there."

I've heard so many stories about this place but never thought I'd ever see it. There's nothing in it right now — no furniture, no toys on the floor — but with every memory my dad mentions, the room slowly starts filling up.

"That's where the floor pillows were. We'd eat breakfast and dinner with plates in our lap and a cup of juice on the floor."

How'd they do it? How did they manage to live here for over a year with a newborn baby and no money?

"We smoked so much weed sitting on those floor pillows."

"Daddy!"

"What? We did. You knew that. Your mom loved smoking. I thought she'd have a problem quitting when she got pregnant but she never took a single puff until weeks after you were born."

"She didn't breastfeed me, right?"

"Naw, you were on formula from day one. Formula and cornmeal porridge. Let's just say you were a healthy-looking child."

"You mean I was a fat child."

Dad nudges me on my arm and I grab hold of his.

"As shitty as this place looks, this was your first home. It was our first home. And that lady upstairs, her name is Elaine. She was a freaking angel, trust me."

Every time I hear the word angel, I automatically think of wings, but I never think of them flying. I think of angels as protectors who wrap their wings around your body and make sure the world doesn't break you. They're as real as bulletproof vests.

"Why'd you bring me here?" I hope that didn't sound like an attack. Like I don't want to be here. I do. But my dad didn't go through all of this trouble to set up this visit for no reason.

"Let's go upstairs."

Cups of black coffee are laid out on a glass center table in Elaine's living room. The young boy is lying on the floor on his stomach watching something on a laptop with headphones covering both ears. Family pictures hang from the walls in uneven rows — Elaine and three young women, Elaine and the young boy, all three women at different ages — stories told in stills, some of which are black-and-white with a younger Elaine adding the color those images need.

A bowl that looks like a genie lamp is holding the cream and a silver spoon is sitting in a small glass bowl of white sugar.

"It look the same down there?"

"It does," my dad says. "You don't rent it out anymore?"

"You and her mother were the only people I ever rented it out to. The girls used to love being down there causin' whatever kinda trouble they caused. After you left, I kept it empty. Never really cared to fill it up again."

"I don't think I knew that."

"How would you? Only thing you cared about when you moved into that basement was surviving."

"Got that right."

The young boy shuts the laptop and flips through the channels on the TV sitting on a wide, black stand. I'm mixing three spoons of sugar and a healthy dose of cream in my coffee.

"This is the first time I've brought her back here," Dad says. "I've told her stories but she's never actually seen it. Not even the outside."

"You moved on," Elaine says. "It's what you're supposed to do. That's how you survive in this world." She looks at me for what feels like the first time. "Sorry about your mother, dear. I lost my mother right after having my first baby. I know it's not easy."

Wow, my dad really has been planning this for a while. I wonder how much he told her.

"Thank you," I say, before taking a long sip.

"My mother was a piece of work, too. Bit of a cunt if you ask me."

I look at my dad, who doesn't look surprised. My cup's down on the table now. "A cunt, you say?"

"Oh yeah. Not a tender bone in her body. She whipped me like a racehorse. Told me I'd never be nothin' and shouldn't even try. I ran out of that house soon as I found a boy ready to take me in."

"You and her weren't speaking when she died?" Dad asks.

"We talked every now and then. She was excited about having a grandbaby. Said it was my chance to do something good in this world."

The curtains pulled wide open against the front windows are touching the floor. Through the windows, I see the other homes across the street, some shaded by tall trees and others brightened with manicured lawns. The evening light flooding into Elaine's home colors our faces like pastel paintings. She's enjoying this, I think. Talking, I mean. She's a storyteller like most grandparents, and regardless of what the stories are about, there's some joy in her tone.

"I'll tell you one thing, though. I cried like a baby when she died. Didn't matter that I didn't want her in my life, didn't matter that she treated me like an inmate my whole childhood, I bawled like I lost a leg."

My dad really is something. We haven't spoken about my mom dying since that argument. Not a word. But here we are, in the house that was my first home, listening to the angel who would later tell me that she let my mom and dad move in without paying first and last month's rent. Who's telling me now that her mother died without them being on the best of terms.

"I didn't even go to my mom's funeral," I say, searching Elaine's face for a reaction, for some kind of shock or disgust or "what kind of child would skip their mother's funeral" type of look.

"You probably did the right thing," she says. "Funerals aren't for the dead, they're for the living. And you're the one gotta live with that person not being here however you can and on your time. You going or not going to your mother's funeral don't mean a damn thing to her. She's already gone somewhere else."

Am I smiling right now? Because I shouldn't be. I know my dad isn't smiling at all. This definitely isn't part of his plan. It can't be. But I want to tell Elaine thank you. That she's right about almost everything she just said, except that I care more about where my mom had been than where she is now. That thought feels wrong, though. It feels like I'm betraying something. Some kind of pact I was forced into at birth because I didn't get to choose whose womb I came out of.

"So you don't see anything wrong with that?" Dad says. "You just said you cried like a baby when you found out your mom died."

"You bet I cried. Then my little girl needed a bottle and all that cryin' was over with." My dad can't look at me. "She wouldn't have been no better a grandmother than she was a mother. I cried because something in my body told me to. Once I got that outta me, I had a life to go live and wasn't wastin' any more of it thinkin' about that lady."

It's almost dark when I give Elaine a long hug on our way out.

"Don't go all mushy on me," she says. Dad bends and puts one arm around her and we're back in the car.

"She was nice," I say.

"That's Elaine. She only knows how to be herself."

Dad pulls up to a stop sign and starts tapping on the steering wheel.

"We have one more stop," he says.

"Okay, I guess I'm canceling with Derrick. Where to now? Back down memory lane again?"

Dad's still tapping the steering wheel and we still haven't pulled away from the stop sign.

"Dad. You there? The sign says stop, not stay."

"Yeah, I'm here," he says. "Put your seatbelt on."

We finally pull out and Dad's taking his time through the side streets. I was only in this neighborhood for the first year of my life. None of the names on these street signs mean anything. None of the turns take me anywhere; seeing swings in the parks doesn't stir any nostalgia.

"We never had a baby shower," my dad says.

"Huh?"

"A baby shower. Your mom and I never had one when she was pregnant with you."

"Why not?"

"Good question, especially since we could've used all the help we could get. But you already know that none of our parents were happy about the pregnancy, and even some of my friends tried to talk me out of it. Said I should convince your mom to have an abortion. When your mom heard that, she said no baby shower. She didn't want any bad energy around when she was pregnant. Plus we were teenagers, so it's not like any of our friends was buying us a stroller."

"I guess that makes sense."

"Yeah, it makes sense now. We argued about it, though. I thought we should at least have a couple people over. Your mom wasn't having it."

The rain isn't even a drizzle anymore so we crack our windows just enough to let the breeze in. We're on the brink of nightfall. With the roads still wet and headlights starting to brighten, it almost feels like we're in some kind of illusion.

"Okay, where you taking me for real, Dad. Why all the secrecy?"

"We're here."

"We're here? Here where?"

We're parked in front of an entrance where it's too dark for me to make out what's on the other side, but as soon as I see that it's an open field, my fists clench and I press my head against the top of the car seat.

"Get me outta here."

"Just hold on, Coi. I —"

"No! No hold on, no come on, Coi, no nothing. Just put the car in reverse and get me out of here."

"I need you to listen to me for one minute, Coi. Just one minute."

I whip my head around to face my dad. "What were you thinking? Really, Dad? What did you think was gonna happen? That I'd stand beside her grave and give a Shakespearean soliloquy about why I regret not going to her funeral and how I'm sorry she's gone?"

"No, that's not what I thought at all."

My phone is out and I'm pressing Confirm on an Uber.

"You have three minutes."

"Really, Coi? That's how you're gonna talk to your father?"

"Looks like they're moving fast. I'd hurry up if I were you."

My dad takes a long, aggravated breath and turns his attention outside his window. He knew this was a possibility. Actually, he must've known that this was a probability. No way he thought that I would ever be okay with this, so what's his real endgame here? Because it couldn't have been me getting out of this car and walking through that cemetery.

"Listen, I didn't expect you to stand by her grave. That's not what this is about."

"So what is it about?"

"We saw Elaine's house, right? That's where everything started. It's where your mother's journey as a parent started. This place. This cemetery. This is where it ended, but there's so much about your mom's life that you don't know. There's almost eighteen years of memories and experiences, and I know most of what you remember is bad, but maybe there's something else."

Uber's already telling me that I should be outside. I hit Cancel and think about how much my rating is going to drop.

"Why are you doing this? You hated my mom. You went to court to get full custody of me before she gave me up on her own. Why does it matter how I feel about her now? Because I don't feel any different. I feel the same way I did when she was alive and didn't care about seeing me."

"You're right. I really didn't like her. But at one point, I loved her. I really did. And I think it's important for you to know that."

"You guys were like seventeen when you met. I couldn't even think about loving someone right now."

"Not even Derrick?"

"Not anyone. It's just too much . . . emotion."

"And that's exactly why we're here. That right there. You can play tough all you want, but I know you, Coi. I know you better than anyone on this planet. And not having your mother in your life affected you in ways you're not even recognizing."

This is more agonizing than a therapy session (which I haven't been to since after the funeral). All of this emotional guidance, as if I can't process my own feelings. I know how I feel. It's just not what everyone wants me to feel.

"Just think about it, Coi. Think about what your mother meant to you and what she means to you now. That's all I'm saying."

My dad puts the car in reverse and pulls out. My headphones are in the entire ride home, although the sound is so low I can barely hear the music. I catch my dad sneaking peeks over at me and by the time we're halfway home, I want to tell him that it's okay. That I get it. I get why he did all this. And if I were him, I'd probably do the same thing.

Still no words by the time we park and walk in the house. It feels like it should be midnight but it's barely ten o'clock. My room is its regular chaos and all I can think about is sinking under those blankets. Normally I'd take a bath first, a hot one, but I fall like a tumbling tree onto my back, the mattress breaking my fall, and stay there.

There.

Here.

There's never really an escape for me. Sometimes my room feels like a fortress and other times it feels like a prison. Nothing in. Nothing out. Just me alone with my thoughts, even though I tell Jes almost everything and even though Derrick's been that blanket I can disappear under without having to say a word.

I regret canceling with him tonight. Maybe I should text him right now and tell him to come by. He'd listen to me rant about how shitty the end of the evening was and nod when he agreed with me and not say anything when he didn't. He'd get a kick out of Elaine, and I can already picture him trying to maneuver around my feelings because God forbid he say the wrong thing and I take whatever I'm feeling right now out on him.

As tempting as that sounds, that yawn tells me it's time to close my eyes. And so I do. And I doze. Further. Deeper. Until I'm finally here.

MY MOTHER'S FACING A BLANK WALL WHEN SHE appears. I'm only steps behind her, but somehow it feels like she's in a different place. Like I'm watching her on a screen instead of from in the same room. I take a step back and she gets closer.

Maybe I'm just out of practice.

That would make sense. I haven't had any dream that I remembered since the last one. None at all. I tried, though. With every ounce of guilt I had in me, I tried. I smoked weed right before bed because I figured it would stimulate my mind. When that didn't work, I tried shrooms. Then meditation, alcohol, reading the Bible; I even tried talking to myself out loud. Still nothing.

So I stopped trying, but those memories of our dream conversations taunted me. It was like the ghost of my mother was whispering in my ear, reminding me of what was, what could've been, what never could be. This went on for weeks.

And now here she is, or here we are, together again in the only way we can be.

"Long time," she says.

"Yeah, but what's time anyway, right? Especially for you." My mom still hasn't turned around but I see her nodding her head. "What's it like?"

There's nothing in this space. No walls I can recognize, no boundaries high or low. It's like we're in some kind of abyss. Paradiso or Inferno? I can't tell.

"Today's that day, isn't it?" she says. "It's why you're here."

"I don't know why I'm here. I don't know why any of this is happening."

"But it's happening." My mom turns around but now we're farther apart. "And I'm glad it is because I miss you."

"That doesn't even make sense," I say. "You don't miss me, you miss life. You haven't seen me in . . ."

The number of days start spinning through my mind. Days I told myself no longer matter. The day my mother left me was the first day I started counting. Now she's left the earth and those days don't make any sense. How can the number of days mean anything when there's no end in sight? No equation that will bring the counting to an end or produce any kind of answer?

"When are you gonna let go?" my mom says.

"Let go of what? I'm not holding on to anything."

We're not so far away from each other that I can't see her grin. It's that same grin she put on when she dropped me off on my first day of kindergarten and I wouldn't let go of her leg. That same grin I imagined when she called me for the first time after all those years and I actually answered.

"You're smarter than that, Coi."

"Really? How do you know that?"

We're close enough now that I can see the length and curve of her eyelashes.

"There it is," she says, "all still inside of you." My mom holds out both hands. "You ready to let go?"

I'm not ready for anything.

I'm not ready . . .

I'm not . . .

"Coi. Coi, wake up. It's okay."

I hear those words repeated over and over again then feel the push of my dad.

"Hey, you okay? I heard you screaming from the living room. Bad dream?"

How loud must I have been for Dad to actually come into my room? To be staring at me like I had a panic attack in my sleep? His hand moves across my forehead and I can feel the sweat wipe away in his palm.

"Don't think I've seen that happen before. Did you, umm . . . did you have one of those dreams?"

"What time is it?" It's still dark out, which isn't making sense. I was sleeping, right? I dreamt that, didn't I?

"It's just after midnight. You haven't been sleeping that long."

My mind feels like a wave that's slowly coming to tide. I see my dad now. See that I'm still in bed. I'm present enough to sit up, rub my eyes and wipe the sweat from my forehead myself.

"Yeah . . . yeah it was one of those dreams."

Dad nods his head and looks away. I open my mouth to tell him that I'm alright. That this is no big deal, just a dream that I need to remember how to control. But I stop myself. For these few seconds, there's no sound at all. No footsteps, not that sound when you shift on your bed, no deep breathing, nothing. The light in my room feels louder than anything, and when my dad turns back toward me I can see that he's silencing himself, too.

"There's something you need to fix, Coi. Something's just not right and you need to figure out what it is."

———

I'm staring at my ceiling the next morning, my eyes heavy but certain. It took me hours to fall back asleep, but when I did, I fell all the way. It still feels too early. My door is wide open and I can hear the muffled conversation of my dad downstairs on what's likely a video call. By the time I make my way down, he's taking out his earphones.

"How you feeling?"

"Good. Better, I guess."

"You sure? That doesn't sound so . . ."

"I'm moving out." Saying it so abruptly, I even surprise myself. As I wait for my dad's reaction, I'm talking to myself so I can actually get through this standing up.

"What do you mean you're moving out?"

"I mean I'm moving out now. Like this week." I take one long, deep breath and step toward my dad. "Listen, everything is not okay. I see that now. I can actually say those words and not feel like I'm failing or something. And I don't know exactly what's wrong but I know I need to figure this out on my own."

"That's the opposite of what you need, Coi. You need support. You need people you can talk to when things get too crazy."

"I'm not running away, Dad. And I know you're always gonna be here for me. You always have been. But what I'm going through isn't a family problem. We were never really a family, or at least I've never felt like that. This is something I need to figure out on my own, wherever that leads me."

"What do you mean we're not a family. You and me, me and you. Of course we're a family. And you just got done your first year of college, Coi. You're still eighteen. Plus we just moved into this new townhouse. I'm doing this for you. Why would you wanna move out now?"

As long as I've been thinking about doing this, as long as I've been planning this, I knew this would be the hardest part. How many times did my dad lie to my mom so I could stay an extra day with him? I was about nine the last time I remember throwing a fit when he tried telling me to get ready.

"We have to go, princess. I was supposed to drop you off this morning."

I was in a mood that day, sitting defiantly on the couch with my arms and legs crossed, snot bubbling out of my nose and tears covering my face.

"No, I'm not going home. I'm staying here with you."

Dad had a small, one-bedroom apartment back then. He'd sleep on the couch whenever I came over and tell me that his room was my room. My clothes took up a small part of his closet and I had two of my own drawers, one of them filled with crayons, pencil crayons and markers, most of them out of their original box and jumbled in a large, silver tin that used to hold chocolate-covered cookies.

"Okay, okay," Dad said, "how about this. How about if

you go to your mom's today, I promise that one day soon, you won't ever have to go back there again?"

"You're lying, Daddy."

"No, look." He held out his pinky and I wiped away some of my tears. "I pinky swear that before you get to high school, it's gonna be me and you."

I unfolded my arms and looked down at my dad's pinky. My nose was still dripping but the crying slowed all the way down.

"You promise?"

"Pinky promise. And we don't break pinky promises, remember?"

To this day, I can't figure out why my dad said that. How did he know? He couldn't have known. Was he already plotting three, four years ahead? He obviously couldn't predict that my mom would walk me out of her home and into his car and never see me again, but he made that promise with so much confidence, so much certainty that I almost think he forced the universe to believe him.

Now we're standing in the kitchen of our second home together and I'm telling him that it can't just be us anymore. In some ways this moment was inevitable. All children move on at some point, right? Start their own lives, maybe have their own families. I know none of those inevitabilities are making my dad feel any better, but I'm trying to get through this minus the snot bubbles.

"Where you gonna move to? And how are you going to afford it?"

"Derrick's mom has an apartment that's not too far from here. She said she mostly lets her friends stay there when they're visiting from out of town, or sometimes she'll stay there when

Derrick's away at camp or something and she doesn't wanna be alone in their mansion. She's letting me stay there till the end of the summer and not charging me anything except maintenance fees, which is like six hundred dollars."

"And you're gonna live there on your own?"

"Yes, Dad. Just me. No one else."

Dad's about to rev up with a million more questions and none of the answers are going to make any difference.

"Listen, I've thought about this. I've been thinking about this since the funeral. And I don't know if it's the right thing to do but I still need to do it. You get that, right?"

His little girl. I bet that's what he's thinking. All grown up. I hope that even though he's probably fighting a minor heart attack right now, some part of him is proud.

"I need to talk to Derrick's mom about this first."

"I know. I'll try to make her call you today."

"And there are gonna be rules . . ."

"Dad!"

He can't help himself. It's like I'm letting go of his hands and he's trying to squeeze mine even tighter.

"Come here."

He pulls me in and hugs me like I'm still that nine-year-old girl crying on his couch.

"Okay, Dad. Let's get through this dry-faced." I try to pull away but he tightens his arms around me.

"Just a little bit longer."

Just a little bit longer. What's time, anyway?

July

HEADPHONES ON. VOLUME HIGH. MY FAVORITE Tyler, The Creator playlist is all I want to listen to.

"Who Dat Boy."

"Lumberjack."

"Earfquake."

There's only one way to listen to Tyler and that's all the way up. I'm sitting at the table in the center of my living room, laptop open, working on a graphic design project for a new client. She wants a full website done, including a logo, and I'm getting Jes to do all the copy, so we're both winning on this one.

I'm still choosing between #DC143C, which is like crimson, and #FF7F50, which is closer to orange, as the primary color. The logo was a breeze. When I showed it to the client she replied, *You're worth every dollar.* Better believe I am. Every damn dollar.

Derrick should be over soon so I need to wrap this up. I'm taking him to his first fashion show and need some time to get dressed. Don't ask me what I'm wearing. All I know is that I want to look extra cute today, or any day that me and

Derrick go out. I like the way he looks at me when I'm all dressed up. Sometimes being arm candy isn't such a bad thing. Plus maybe if I'm all done up, he won't pressure me about staying at my apartment. I've barely been here for a month and he's been bugging me for a key the whole time. Boys are funny, but he's a keeper so I'm just letting him be. I still smile every time I say no. And he asks again and I smile again. He's persistent, I'll give him that. Patient and persistent.

Even though I haven't been here for long, this place feels like mine. I didn't change any of the furniture that was already here, didn't move anything around or try to make this place feel like me. It's like it was designed precisely for my taste.

The first thing I did when my dad dropped me off was belly flop on the bed. My arms and legs were fully stretched and I still couldn't cover the majority of that king-sized mattress. When I rolled over on my back, I folded my hands together and told God thank you like a million times. I still couldn't believe Lucy did this for me.

I put out the joint I was smoking and hop in the shower. I'm still getting dressed when I hear Derrick knock so I just unlock the door and hustle back to my room.

"I'm ready," I yell.

"Really, because there's still steam coming out of the bathroom."

"That's not steam."

He slides open the room door just as I'm buttoning up my leather pants.

"See? Ready."

A girl I met in my summer merchandising course was the one who told me about the fashion show, which is also an art party. She actually surprised me with two tickets on the last day of summer classes, which is really what I love the most about college. I meet people who love fashion just as much as I do and know what's happening around the city. I've made so many connections just in my first year and it's opened up this whole new world for me. I'm probably too young to be at a lot of the parties I get invited to, but the fashion and art communities in Toronto are small, and once you're in, you're in. No one cares that I'm not legally old enough to drink.

This particular party is downtown on John Street, at a loft that I've been to before for a pop-up shop. It's a cool space wide enough for sections of couches against brick walls. Last time I was there, the DJ and bartender were near the back and racks of clothes occupied the middle of the floor. I'm guessing that's where the models will walk this time, or at least that's how I'd do it. Whenever I actually decide to do it.

I'm still figuring out how to plan my first runway show. I don't even know if I want it to be a runway show. It's not like I have thirty pieces to show off, plus I had this idea of just hanging the designs like artwork. Not against the wall, but from like a string or something so it looks like the clothes are floating. Maybe. I don't know. We'll see how that goes. I'm hoping to get some inspiration tonight.

"How do I look?" I switched out the leather pants for baggy jeans and a vintage crop top. It's paired with three gold necklaces and hoop earrings and I just know Aaliyah would be proud.

"Like my girl." He tries wrapping his arm around my waist and I shove him away.

"D, seriously. Do I look good or what?"

"When do you ever not look good?"

"You're no help."

Derrick disappears from the room and comes back with a small box wrapped in a red ribbon.

"What's this for?"

"Open it."

Derrick spins me around and we're both in front of my floor mirror. He rests his chin on my shoulder and kisses my cheek. As I take my time unwrapping the box, I'm thinking of what it is this time. Last time, he bought me earrings that looked way too expensive to wear to school, so I've only worn them once or twice. He's given me front-row tickets to Raptor games and a set of charcoal pencils. This box looks super fancy, though, and I know he's not dumb enough to buy me a ring so I'm taking my time to savor the moment.

When I open the box and see the white-gold necklace and pendant with my initials on it, I close it shut.

"Where did you get this?"

"You don't like it?" He sounds more confused than disappointed.

"I said where did you get this?"

I pull away and now we're face-to-face.

"If you don't like it just say so. I'll take it back and get something different. I just thought . . ."

"What did you think? Why would you get me this?" I toss the box on my bed and now both hands are on my hips.

"Chill. I saw a picture of you at your dad's house when you were younger. You had the exact same necklace on. I never saw you wear it so I thought you lost it or something. Figured I'd buy you one that looked just like it."

I should just break up with this guy. Tell him it's over and that I never want to see him again. But even though I haven't been to therapy in months, I know this is an extreme thought that I don't need to turn into an extreme action. Instead, I shove Derrick out of the bedroom.

"Just wait out there. I'll be done in a minute."

———

The first shot of tequila burns my chest. The models haven't come out yet but the DJ's spinning all the best trap shit. On the way over, I basically sat in the corner of the Uber and stared out the window for the full fifteen-minute ride. Derrick didn't say anything either but he kept rubber-necking to see if I'd crack and actually tell him what that necklace means. He was probably wondering what was going through my head. That maybe I was deep in thought about what happened at my apartment. What I was really thinking about was what kind of tequila they had at the bar. I'm usually a sip-a-glass-of-wine-for-the-whole-night type of girl, but I need something to fix my mood tonight and sipping slow isn't going to cut it.

Once we got here, I beelined to the bar and now I'm ready for my second shot.

"Are we gonna talk about this?"

"There's nothing to talk about." I hand Derrick a shot, tap his glass and bottoms-up again. "Let's just enjoy the show."

Six rows of chairs are spread on either side of a bright blue carpet. Most people are gathered in small friend groups around high tables that are littered around the perimeter of the room. I order a mixed drink and we manage to find an empty high table.

"It's your mom, right? She bought you that necklace. That's why you're tripping out?"

Maybe if I sip this drink slowly, he'll get the point. Or maybe I should throw it at him. *Extreme thought, Coi, extreme thought.*

"Okay, I get it. My bad. But how could I have known?"

Maybe if I down this whole drink, he'll shut up. Actually, I have a better idea. I walk to his side of the table, grab his chin and splash our lips together.

"It's all good, D. I've already forgotten about it." Derrick leans in for another kiss and I wrap my arms around his neck and let him have it. Boys are so easy. "You ready for another shot now?"

We take two more shots and I down a mixed drink before the show is about to start. We're sitting at the edge of the back row now, and I have some kind of tequila mixed drink in my hand. I'm feeling a little wavy but the room isn't spinning so I must still be good. When the first model hits the stage, I start clapping.

"Wooo, work it girl."

Derrick looks at me but doesn't say anything. The other models start walking out and it's like they're my models and this is my show and I need to make sure they know they're killing it right now. When the third model gets to the end of the runway and twirls around before walking back, I shoot to my feet.

"Yes! Yes, yes, yes. Do your thing, girl."

Heads start glaring backward. Some of the models look over at me and try their best to stick to the task. Derrick gets up, grabs my hand and walks me to the exit. I'm still cheering till we get outside.

"What the fuck are you doing?" Derrick screams.

"I'm having a good time. You should try it."

"That's what you call a good time? Do you know what you were doing in there?"

"It's better than talking about some stupid necklace."

"I thought you were over it?"

I can't. I really can't. Not right now. Not ever, really. I'm ready to tell Derrick all the ways he's fucking up. I want to tell him that all of this is pointless because that's just what it is with me. But my stomach feels like a lava pit and now there are two Derricks standing in front of me. I stumble over to the closest wall and heave out all those tequila shots. A few seconds later, more vomit projectiles out. Derrick's right beside me rubbing my back and telling me that it's okay. Not to worry about it because everything's okay.

The next time I open my eyes, we're in front of my apartment getting out of a taxi. Derrick's holding me up, through the front doors, up the elevator.

"I'm sorry, D. I'm so sorry." Who knows how many times I say that before Derrick lays me down on my bed and takes off my sneakers.

"How bad was it?" I ask. He chuckles.

"Go to sleep, Coi. I'll be here when you wake up."

ME AND MY SISTER ARE CLOSE ENOUGH TO THE kitchen that we can hear the water boiling in wide pots on the stove. Plantain and sweet potato in one, dumplings on their own in the other. I'm coloring in a picture of a house that I drew that's due the next day. The teacher told us to draw our perfect home and so my house had a pointy roof with three bedrooms and a chimney like in some of the books we read in class. When I showed it to my teacher the next day, she asked me, "Where are the people?"

Kayla is still a toddler, always close by, always up to something. I can see her crawling under the table then running through the kitchen before our mother tells her to stay out. Two lamps on either side of the couch are the only light in the living room, and the lampshade makes our apartment feel like it's always sunset.

"Do you remember this?" I ask my dream mother. It's the first lucid dream I've had since the day I told my dad I was moving out. The irony that this happens on a night where I'm barely lucid in real life isn't lost on me. "Do you know what's about to happen?"

I'm on the floor, legs crossed with the sheet of paper in front of me.

"Why are you doing this?" my dream mom asks. "Why is it always these memories?"

The saltfish on the stove smells like Sunday morning. It's the dish I went to sleep thinking about every weekend. Then, when Sunday came and I woke up to my mom in the kitchen slicing tomatoes and chopping green onions, my mouth watered like the mouths of most kids my age would at the sight of ice cream or some kind of candy.

"Why am I doing this? Are you serious? These are my memories, which means this stuff really happened. So I'm not doing anything. You've already done it."

The pendant from my gold chain is dangling just slightly as I lean over to fill in another color. The fridge door opens and closes and I know without looking back that my mom just pulled out the carrot juice. Cupboards open and close, so do the drawers.

"But there's more, Coi," my dream mother says to me. "There's more than just all this. This can't be all you remember."

My mom asks me to set the table. Dave pops out of the room like he's been waiting to hear those words the whole time. He takes his regular seat at the head of the table while I set his plate in front of him. My mom's right behind me with the ackee and saltfish in hand with serving spoons in each dish.

"There is more," I say. "Keep watching."

She lifts a spoonful into Dave's plate, then another half before Kayla pops up from under the table and crawls under my legs. Her rubbing against my calves startles me and I

115

back into my mother. The serving dish doesn't crack when it hits the floor, but the ackee and saltfish are spread in a neat pile along the tiles.

It's still for a moment. Even Kayla stops crawling and acknowledges the spill.

"You know what's about to happen, right, Mom? You know what you're about to do?"

Dave walks to the kitchen counter to grab a roll of paper towels.

"You, get out of here," my mom says to Kayla. "And you." She turns to me with fury in her eyes. "Can you try not to be so fucking clumsy?"

"Relax, Crissy," Dave says. "It was an accident. I'm 'bout to clean it up right now." She ignores Dave and keeps her rage focused on me.

"Do you see how much food you just wasted? You know that cost money, right?"

I'm not who I am yet. My mother's words still make me shiver and I keep my eyes pinned to my feet. Dave's already lifted the first pile. "Look at me when I'm talking to you." She says that while forcing my chin up to meet her glare. "I said you know that cost money, right?"

"Yes, Mommy."

"And none of us in here have money to waste so why you wasting our money?"

"Crissy, leave the girl alone. It's not that serious."

"Stay out of this. I'm talking to my daughter right now." Dave shakes his head and carries another pile to the trash. My mom grabs both my cheeks and squeezes till my face looks like a bad selfie meme.

116

"You have something you wanna say to me?" The first tears slip down my face. "That's the problem. You don't value anything. You think this house don't cost money? You think those couches and your crayons don't cost money? You think that necklace around your neck is free?"

She lets go of my face and traces her finger around the front of the necklace.

"Is that what you think? That this is free?"

My mother tugs on the chain with so much force that it pops off my neck and I tumble to the ground.

"When you learn to value things, I'll give this back to you." She walks off. I'm on my hands and knees, heaving. Kayla crawls toward me and holds on to my arm.

"WAKE UP, SLEEPYHEAD."

It's not the voice I expected. Jes is sitting on the side of my bed with a cup of water and what I'm guessing are two extra-strength Advils.

"I heard you had a night." I sit up and swallow both pills with one sip.

"Where's D?"

"He had to go. It's like lunchtime, girl. You've been out for a minute. He messaged me a bit ago and asked if I could come by till you woke up."

The memories from last night's show come flooding back but are mixed with the nightmare of last night's dream. I sink back into bed and cover my face with my pillow.

"Ugh, I can't do this."

"Can't do what? Drink? We already knew that."

I sit back up and think about how much to share with Jes. Should I tell her about this dream? About why I was really mad at Derrick last night? I know I can trust her, but I'm starting to doubt myself. These dreams or visions or whatever the heck they are might have taken a break, but they're not going away.

"You know I'm your best friend, right, Coi?"

"I know."

"So tell me why you got so drunk that you were cheering on the models like you were at a Raptors game."

I don't even know why I hesitate with this girl. I break down everything, starting with the chain Derrick bought me and ending with my dream. Jes is vaping and nodding the whole time.

"I moved out of my dad's house to figure things out on my own. You know, like figure my shit out so I can feel like a normal human for five minutes."

"You left your dad's house because you're a runner." Jes shoves me over and gets into bed with me. "I love you, girl. You know that. But you're a runner. That's how you deal. Whenever there's a problem, you either hide or you run. That's how you've always been, at least since I've known you."

"You think I'm running?"

"I mean, you're here, right? In bed hungover when you could've just told Derrick about why that necklace was triggering. Just like you could've stayed at your dad's house but you knew he'd pressure you to deal with your feelings toward your mother. Same reason you don't see your therapist anymore. And for real, Coi, you know you should've went to your mom's funeral. I know all the reasons you told me and it all makes sense, but that doesn't make it right. You should've went. I think you know that."

Jes is patting me like a puppy while she says all this but I still want to tell her that she doesn't know what she's talking about. That I'm not running, I'm giving myself space. I'm not hiding, I just need to figure things out on my own time.

119

But as much sense as those reasons made before, they sound like excuses now. Like I made it all up like one of my designs.

"You think that's why I'm having these dreams?"

"I don't know. Those dreams are weird. But it makes sense that they're happening because of some kinda unresolved thing that you're going through."

"Yeah, I think so, too. But I don't even know what to do, Jes. Like where do I even start with this thing? The person I need closure from is dead."

Jes pulls out her phone and starts scrolling.

"But you still talk to her, right? Whatever weird kinda dream thing is going on, you're talking to your mom, so talk to her. Don't just show her all the bad stuff she's done to you, give her a chance to talk. Maybe explain some things."

Jes hands me her phone.

"Look at this. I've been watching these videos. This lady, she talks about forgiveness and trauma and stuff like that. Check out some of the clips right now. In that one right there, she says that you don't forgive someone or try to get over your trauma for the person that caused it, you do it for yourself. And you don't even need that other person to be part of your healing journey. It's really all about you."

I'm DMing all of these clips to my IG.

"Watch those," she says, "and get your butt up and go take a shower."

I'M STANDING ON THE OTHER SIDE OF THE STREET staring at Elaine's house. Seeing it under a bright summer sun doesn't make it look as archaic as I remembered it. I see the charm now, even if part of that is because I know who's inside.

I'm still trying to figure out what I'm doing here though. I know that dream I had last week did something to me. Reliving that memory felt like being broken all over again, and after Jes left that afternoon, I felt motivated to start putting those broken pieces back together. My dad was right — something needs fixing. Not something, me. I need fixing. And I have a feeling that fixing starts here. But how? What questions do I want answered and why do I think Elaine can answer them? All I know is that this is where my life started. It's also the last place my mom and dad were together. That has to mean something.

When I finally take enough breaths to cross the street, Elaine's screen door opens.

"It's about damn time. I thought you were gonna stand over there the whole day."

She's in a burgundy sweat suit with white sneakers and moving swiftly down her driveway.

"Follow me to the basement," she says. "Nice jeans. I remember the days I could've pulled those off."

The basement is still empty. Elaine disappears behind a door I didn't notice my first time here and comes out with two jars of sauce.

"Homemade. You hungry?"

"Sure." She sets the two jars down beside the sink and leans against the counter.

"You know, your mom really knew how to cook. Everything she made tasted like a little slice of heaven. She'd come upstairs and ask me for all kinds of spices, then come back up an hour later with a plate of something I never ate in all my life."

"I remember that. Not here, of course, but I remember her cooking. When I went to school, my mom made me these sandwiches with chicken and coleslaw and tomato. And not like deli meat chicken. These were jerk chicken sandwiches you'd get at a Jamaican restaurant on Eglinton or something. My friends always wanted a bite, so my mom started making me two so I could give one away."

I hear the thumps from her grandson running or jumping upstairs. Elaine rolls her eyes and brushes past me to the other side of the kitchen.

"See that vent up there? We told your mom and dad to keep that thing closed when they got to smoking. The smell came straight upstairs to the living room. Every time I smelled it, I'd give a couple bangs and they'd close it right up."

"How often did you have to bang?"

"More often than I shoulda been."

Elaine picks up the two jars of sauce and motions for me to follow her upstairs.

"Did you talk to my mom a lot when she lived here?"

"We spoke enough. She was so young that we really didn't have much to talk about. Most of the time, she'd be sittin' on the porch right there or in the kitchen listening to me tell my stories. I know she was a handful, but to me, she was always just a kid."

I've heard my mom described as "just a kid" so many times it makes me want to gag.

"How can she have known what she was doing? She was just a kid."

"You're being too hard on her. She was just a kid."

"Give her a break. She was just a kid."

Elaine stops walking and turns around.

"What do you want, dear? What you looking for? You came here for a reason so get to it."

I can't wait to get old so I can say whatever the heck I want and no one take it personal. Elaine's stare is challenging me to say something. Daring me to. She knows. She knows what I want to hear, what I need to hear. Why won't she just tell me?

"I don't know," I say. "I just thought . . . I don't know what I thought. I'm sorry."

"Don't be sorry," Elaine says and lifts her arms for me to come under. "Everyone says that there's two types of people in the world. That's bullshit. There's only people and we're all the goddamn same. No one better or worse than the other. The only thing that makes us different is what we tell ourselves. So I'll tell you what my mom told me: be careful what you tell yourself."

When we get inside Elaine's kitchen, she pulls a long, glass dish of lasagna out of the oven. Her grandson comes running down the stairs and hops on the dining room chair.

"Hope you're not one of those vegetarians," Elaine says to me. I smile and tell her I'm not.

"Good. Don't understand why people don't eat meat. Then again I don't understand a lot of stuff your generation does."

She places the dish on top of the stove with the steam still rising.

"This thing needs to cool off," she says to her grandson. "Why don't you go back upstairs till I call. Let me and the young lady have some time to chat."

He gets up without a fuss and sprints up the stairs. Elaine sits down and invites me to sit across from her at the same dining table.

"You look so much like your mother. It's like she's the one sitting right here."

"How do you remember so much about my mom? It's been almost twenty years now."

"Your mom is not someone you forget. You can meet her once or a hundred times. Don't matter. You're getting all of her no matter what."

Elaine gets up to grab a bowl of salad out of the fridge.

"Do you remember how she and my dad got along?"

"They didn't. But you already know that." I did know that. I don't even know why I asked. "Listen, dear, I'm an old woman. I'm not gonna be around that much longer. Whatever you wanna know, better ask me now."

I stop my leg from shaking and look straight at Elaine.

"Do you think my mom loved me?" Elaine leans back in her chair and crosses her arms. "I mean, like, was she nice to me? Did she do nice things for me? This is stupid, right?"

"Not stupid at all, dear. I'm just not sure how to answer those questions. Did she do nice things for you? I saw her take you to the park. I saw you laugh when she blew bubbles into your belly. But you wanna know if she loved you. Why wouldn't she? She had you, didn't she?"

Elaine gets up again and grabs three plates from the kitchen cabinet.

"Yeah but just because she made me doesn't mean she ever loved me. You should know what I mean. You said your mom was kinda the same way."

"She was. But if you asked my mother if she loved me, she'd say more than anything in the world." My memory spurs a quick compilation of all the times growing up that I heard my mom say "My kids are everything." It was like her default answer to any choice she made, right or wrong. "But none of that really matters, right? They could say they love us till the sun loses its shine. Don't make any difference if we don't feel it. I know I didn't feel it. And I'm guessing you didn't either."

"I didn't. I mean, sometimes, but not really."

Elaine gets up again and I think she's headed back to the kitchen. Instead, she walks over to my side of the dining table and pulls up a chair right beside me.

"You and me, we have something in common. We both had difficult mothers. The difference between you and me is that I never spent any time thinking about why my mother was the way she was. I'm not saying I didn't wish she was different, but she wasn't. I knew that and did what I had to do to make my life better."

Elaine lifts both of her palms upward.

"Give me your hands," she says. I rest both of my hands in hers and she grips them loosely.

"You're alive, dear. You're young, you're as beautiful as a summer day, and you have a father that loves you more than life. Your mother ain't walking out of that grave anytime soon so what you gonna do?"

I think Elaine is asking me a rhetorical question, but she stops talking and she's staring into my eyes like she's looking for something.

"What you gonna do?" she asks again. "What are you going to do?"

I stay silent and try looking at everything except Elaine. The steam's stopped rising from the lasagna and the cabinet where Elaine got the plates is still open.

"Look at me," she says. "What are you going to do?"

Footsteps running down the stairs turns Elaine's attention away.

"Let's eat."

MY PHONE VIBRATES FROM A NUMBER I DON'T recognize. I'm lying on the couch in my living room draped in one of Derrick's T-shirts with a half-smoked joint pressed in the center of my lips. I click the phone silent and spark the joint back up. I'm barely able to exhale a mouthful of smoke before my phone vibrates again.

I pick up the call without saying a word. If it's urgent enough for them to call me back-to-back, I figure they must have a lot to say.

"Coi, you there?"

"Lady?"

"Who else it supposed to be?" I pop straight up on my couch and out the joint in the ashtray like my grandmother was knocking at the door. "Your aunt tells me you're living by yourself now. True?"

"Yeah, I'm in an apartment on my own."

"Must be nice?"

Maybe it's because I'm a little high or maybe it's because I'm wondering why Lady is calling me for the first time in years, but I ignore her last statement or question or whatever that was and stay silent.

"Alright. Well, I guess you're wondering why I'm calling. The family is having a barbecue next week and I want you to come." My thumb is hovering over the End button. "You going to say something, child?"

"What do you mean 'the family'?"

"I mean *your* family. Your sister, your cousins. You remember you have a family?"

Does she know I'm ready to press End?

"How come Aunty never told me about this barbecue."

"I don't know but she'll be there, too."

I have so many questions. My gut is telling me that this will be a waste of time. That this seemingly spontaneous invitation is really a well-thought-out ploy to get me out so "the family" can pile on me for not coming to my mom's funeral or whatever else I haven't done since I've been with my dad.

"Listen, child, whether you like it or not, you're part of this family. You share the same blood with a lot of us. Where I come from, nothing thicker than blood and nothing more important than family. The invitation is open. Come or don't."

Lady ends the call before I do.

"Barbecue?" I say out loud. My phone's still in my hand so I call Aunty.

"Guess who just called me?"

"Your grandmother. I know."

"So this was planned out?"

"I don't know about planned out. She said she wanted

128

to have a barbecue and asked me if she should invite you. Of course I said yes."

"When did she tell you?"

"Just a little while ago."

I know I'm thinking about this way too hard. My grandmother is inviting me to a family barbecue; there's nothing strange about that. Except that it's Lady and we haven't spoken to each other at all since the hospital. Aunty's been the only bridge. She sent me a text about a week after I didn't show up to my mom's funeral that said, *I'm here whenever you're ready.* Me being me, I didn't reply for a week, and when I did, all I wrote was *TY.*

"Are you gonna come?" Aunty asks.

"I'm thinking about it."

Jes would be wringing my neck right now. She'd probably snatch the phone from me and tell Aunty that I'll be there bright and early when the food's still on the grill.

"You should be there, Coi. Seriously. I know you don't like to be pressured or whatever. You wanna make your own decisions and that's fine. But you should be there. I'm asking you to be there."

How much have I disappointed Aunty? I wonder how often she has to stick up for me.

"Coi is just . . ."

"It's been hard for Coi, too . . ."

"We have to give her space to . . ."

How many times has she had to excuse my behavior to Lady or Dave or my sister?

My sister. I tuck that thought away before it creeps any closer to the surface.

"Okay, Aunty. I'll be there."

Saying those words feels like a pact. There's no going back now. No turning off my phone that day or canceling last minute because "I have a migraine." I told Aunty I'll be there so I'll be there.

———

The week goes by like a Formula 1 race. Derrick and his mom came over on Wednesday. We spent most of our time on the balcony, Lucy taking her time through a bottle of red before passing out on the couch. Me and Derrick stayed up in my room till after two, watching YouTube and talking about music, which is his favorite topic.

I spent Thursday and Friday working on some new designs. I learned this new patchwork technique from this designer I saw on *Next In Fashion* and I'm figuring out how to incorporate that into my collection. At least I think it's a collection. We'll see how long before I change my mind and start completely new designs because something else inspired me.

Come or don't.

There's no choice in those words. And as I'm applying this last bit of eyeliner, I think to myself that Lady better be careful what she wishes for, because here I come. Actually, I should say here we come. Jes is on my couch scrolling through her phone. I asked her to come with me, or told her to, really; either way, she's excited. I would've asked Derrick to come, too, but he and his guy friends went to Blue Mountain for the weekend.

You ever been to a barbecue before? I texted after she agreed.
Duh.
Yeah, but have you ever been to a Black barbecue?
Is there a difference?
Oh, girl.
She sent back like twenty laughing-face emojis.

I need her with me today. I know Aunty's going to be there, but something tells me I'm going to need all the firepower I can carry, and Jes being here with me is like a machine gun.

The barbecue is at Centennial Park, which is in the west end of the city near Lady's apartment. The nostalgia of this place kicks in as soon as I step on the grass. Track and field was the only after-school activity my mom let me do during elementary school, and only because Kenesha was on the team and we lived in the same complex. Kenesha's mom came to all the meets. You couldn't miss her because she'd be running along with us from in front of the stands, pumping her fists and screaming "g'wan, g'wan" over and over till the race was done. She didn't just do that when Kenesha was running; she kept that same enthusiasm when I lined up for the hundred meters or took the baton for the last leg of the relay. She bought us burgers and hot dogs after the meet, then drove us home and told my mom that I was "fast like lightnin' in a storm."

How fast would I have to be to escape this storm? Okay, that's extreme. Nothing's happened yet so I should be more open to the possibility that this barbecue is an opportunity. I get to see Aunty and probably see my sister. I haven't reached out to her at all since before the funeral, and now I don't have my mom to blame for keeping us apart. What am I going to say to her if she's here? What if she doesn't even want to talk to me? I deserve that. I deserve whatever reaction I get from her. These thoughts are sending me into a tailspin so I'd rather focus on Lady and this food we're about to throw down. Lady might be hard to deal with but she can cook her ass off, so I know I'll be eating some finger-licking dishes.

"Hey." Jes holds on to my forearm and turns me toward her. "You're gonna be alright. We're gonna eat some food, listen to some reggae music, and have a good time. Whenever you're ready to go, I'm with you."

I nod my head and bear-hug her. "You're making me all mushy. I'm gonna be just like you soon."

The sound of Capleton howling through the speakers guides us through the park and toward the group. Hints of weed smoke penetrate the scent of jerk pork and what has to be curried goat. Dave is the first person I see, blunt in hand and reaching in the cooler for what I know will be a Guinness.

"I must be really high," he says. "I think I'm seeing a ghost."

"A holy ghost, I hope."

Dave leans in for a hug.

"How you been? Long time since we talked."

"I'm good. I mean . . . you know. I'm surviving." *Out of all the things to say, Coi. Surviving? Really?* "This is my friend Jessica. Jes, this is Dave."

I'm scanning the park while Jes and Dave exchange pleasantries. Aunty's sitting on a chair at the other end with her son on her lap. Pharaoh was breastfeeding last time I saw him and now he's sitting up straight drinking out of a sippy cup. Lady's sitting in the middle of a large picnic table.

She's too far away and the music is too loud for me to hear what she's saying, but everyone at that table is facing her and not saying a word. My sister, though. Where is my sister?

Aunty waves and I start walking over. Jes is right behind me but before we get halfway to Aunty, I hear my name being yelled from the picnic bench. I keep my head straight but stop walking. It's not like I didn't expect this. I'm only here because I was summoned and now it's time for me to take the stand.

I put on my grateful granddaughter face and mosey over. "Hi, Lady."

"Come 'round here let me see you. Long time since I've seen your face." Jes is hovering close like a bodyguard would to a celebrity, but she looks like she just won the high school science fair so I don't think anyone's intimidated. "Lord, look 'pon my grandchild. Pretty like pearls."

My hands are folded behind my back and I haven't stopped pretending to smile.

"Yuh get any food yet? I cook goat, jerk chicken, jerk pork, rice and peas and some oxtail. Go grab a plate. Come find me when you're done."

I still have my pretend smile on when I finally get to Aunty. There aren't any more free chairs so Jes and I sit on the grass.

"I wasn't sure you would come."

"Neither was I. This is Jessica, by the way." Pharaoh is trying to grab Aunty's hair and doesn't respond to our waving. "Where's Kayla?"

Aunty looks down at Pharoah then gently moves his hands.

"She's not here. The last few months have been . . . Kayla's not really dealing with things well."

"What do you mean? Is she okay?" Suddenly I can feel the grass prickling my bum.

"Depends on what you mean by okay. I mean, she lost her mom. Dave said getting her to go to school after that was tough enough, and then the teachers said she just sat in class all day and didn't do or say anything. So Dave had to speak to the principal to get some kind of exemption. She still passed eighth grade but we think high school's gonna be a struggle."

Aunty might as well stick her hand through my chest and rip my heart out. I have so many questions for her, questions I should already know the answers to. Questions I shouldn't even need to ask if I was being a big sister.

Aunty's attention shifts behind me and I don't need to turn around to know Lady is walking this way.

"You still didn't get no food?"

"No, I'm good, Lady. I'll eat soon."

"What about yuh friend?"

"Oh, well, I am a little hungry." Jes looks over at me and I nod to let her know I'll be fine.

"Make sure you try the oxtail," Lady says as Jes heads to the food table.

"I'm gonna grab some food for this kid, too, before he eats his whole arm." Aunty gets up and Lady takes her place on the chair. I'm still sitting on the grass taking silent, deep breaths.

"Did Aunty tell you 'bout Kayla?"

"Yeah, she was just telling me."

"Poor child. She's like a fish out of water now." Lady's gray hair is shining. Normally she covers it with a wig but right now it's in full splendor. I can picture what she looked like in the sixties and seventies, back on the countryside in Jamaica. She doesn't tell many stories of her time back home, or maybe she does. "I can't even imagine what she's going through. Losing a daughter is a hard thing. A hard, hard thing. But to lose your mother when you still need her; you can't blame Kayla for how she's behaving."

"Wait, how is she behaving?"

"You should be ashamed to ask that question. You don't know how your sister is doing?"

I expected that. And she isn't wrong, so there's not much I can say or do except ignore her digs and try to get some answers.

"I know, I know. I haven't been around . . ."

"You haven't been around? This is the first time you've seen your family since your mother was unconscious in the hospital."

Jes and I should've come up with some kind of distress signal. Something to let her know that she needs to save me from this confrontation. I peek off to the side; she and Aunty are having a laugh.

"I know, and I'm sorry. I just . . ."

"You just what? You mean you're just selfish? Immature? What? I know you don't like me and that's fine. I'm your grandmother and I love you even though you think I'm a nasty old lady. But your sister? What she do to you?"

Nothing. Not a damn thing. And yes, I'm selfish. Maybe I'm immature, too. I don't know. But that's the problem, isn't it? Not knowing. At least that's what Lady thinks. I peep over at Jes again and she's stuffing a piece of something in her mouth. Lady's not done.

135

"Nothing to say?" she says. "You want your friend to come save you?"

"I don't need saving, Lady." I stand up and brush the rear of my jeans. "I lost my mom, too, long before Kayla did. So yeah, get mad at me and tell me how whatever my sister is going through is my fault. Nothing you say to me is worse than what I say to myself."

"So what, we should feel sorry for you? That's what you want? Pity? Sympathy? You need to grow up. You think nobody cares about you but you don't give no one a chance to get close enough to care."

We're loud enough now for heads to turn. Aunty and Jes are walking toward us and Lady's still sitting on the chair.

"You think your life and your problems worse than anybody else? Things happen. That's life. But you think you're above suffering."

Now it feels like someone's pressing a hot towel against my shoulder and back.

"You think I want sympathy? From you? Don't kill me. *I* feel sympathy for *you*. My mom's dead and now all of a sudden you're some kind of saint? You didn't know how to be a mother. Mom forced you to be in our lives and you still never showed up. All those fake phone calls, pretending we wanted to talk to you even though we knew you weren't shit."

"Coi!" Aunty rarely raises her voice but her tone cuts through the argument.

"What? She's a bully, Aunty. She's always talking down to me like she's some perfect person. I'm tired of it."

"You, tired of me?" Lady says. "Isn't that something? This family has been tired of you for a long time."

Jes steps in between us and grabs both my hands.

"Coi, let's just go." I know she's right. I should turn around and walk out of here. I've said enough. Maybe too much.

"No. I'm not leaving. This is what you wanted, right, Lady? When you invited me here. This is what you wanted to happen, right? You wanted to get at me. Take me down. Make me feel like shit in front of everyone."

"Coi, let's go!" Jes aggressively spins me around and starts pushing me away from Lady. I don't hear the music anymore.

"This is what you *all* wanted to see, right? Well congratulations. Next time I'll bring some goddamn props."

CONCH FRITTERS AND TOSTONES. THAT'S THE ONLY thing that can solve this right now. Jes and I make our way to the Cuban restaurant two city blocks from my apartment that I treat like a fast-food spot. It's usually open till about 2 a.m. and I've satisfied my late-night cravings here more than once.

It's early evening and there's still plenty of light outside. The outdoor benches are free but I tell Jes that I'd rather be inside and we find a seat at the corner near the kitchen, which is as far back in the restaurant as you can get.

We sit side by side, dipping our conch fritters in a cream sauce that tastes like the clouds and digging into tostones and the accompanying rice and beans, avocado, red cabbage and tomato. We're two tables away from the closest patrons — a small group of girls who look about our age, too busy with themselves to even notice us.

"You know," Jes starts, "you could've at least let me finish that jerk chicken before you went off like that. Or just one more bite of that potato salad. I would've been happy with that."

"You're lucky. I didn't even get to touch a chicken leg."

We came straight here from the barbecue in a silent Uber ride. Just before we pulled up, Jes said to me, "I get it, Coi. I really do."

I couldn't hold back after that. I started sobbing while we were still in the backseat, face in my hands, rocking back and forth like a pendulum. Jes didn't say anything, and when we got to the restaurant she asked the driver to give us a minute.

When I finally pulled myself together, Jes looked at me and said, "So that's what you meant by a Black barbecue."

I laughed till my head hurt. The barbecue was a nightmare, Lady was a horror movie, but I got out alive. I guess all there is to do after that is laugh.

"Should we order more fritters?" I ask Jes.

"Why are you even asking?"

Two men with shaved, graying beards come through the front door holding hands. The server asks if they want to sit inside or out, and they exit to one of the benches.

"I need to message my sister. I'm really fucking that up." Jes nods but doesn't respond. "I don't know. I mean . . . like my grandmother's a bitch but she was right. I am selfish. I didn't do what a big sister should. Her mother died and I disappeared. She must feel like she has nobody."

"She was your mother too, Coi. And it's never too late to try. I think your sister will be happy if you reach out."

"I need to do more than reach out."

The group of girls burst out laughing at a video they're watching on one of their phones. The door rings as more people file in. For some reason I think about my dad. I wonder if I should tell him what happened at the barbecue, but I shut that down as quickly as I thought it up. No one's getting me out of this. Not my dad, not Jes, not Aunty or Derrick. Nobody.

I guzzle down the last bit of milkshake and pick up a hot fritter.

No one's getting me out of this.

"YOU DON'T RECOGNIZE THIS PLACE, DO YOU?" MY
mother's voice is behind me.

"Where is this?" Blue jeans and sweaters are folded neatly
in the closet. Hangers hold belts, plaid shirts and dresses.

"This is my bedroom. It was my bedroom. Give it a
minute, you'll see."

The room door swings open and bangs into the door
stopper. A young girl with my eyes grabs a knapsack and
fills it with whatever she can fit. She grabs another plastic
bag from the floor and fills that, too. Amid the commotion,
I hear slippers stepping on wood; slow, deliberate steps like
the villain in a horror movie who knows that no matter how
fast their victim runs, they won't escape. They can't escape.

The steps come to a stop, and standing in the doorway is
the first thing I recognize. Lady has one hand placed firmly
on her hip and leans the other against the doorframe. She's
draped in a white nightgown, her hair wrapped tightly in a
purple-and-gold head tie.

"Is this making sense now?" My mom asks. She's beside
me, watching me watch this scene play out. I can't take my

eyes off the room, off of Lady standing resonant, almost threatening, though she hasn't said a word.

The young girl snatches some kind of jewelry off the dresser and now she's face-to-face with Lady.

"I'm not coming back this time," she says. "You want me gone, I'm gone, but this is it."

Lady glares down at the young girl. I know that look too well. I've just seen it, just survived it. Lady doesn't have to say anything to cut you down, to make you question, in that moment, every choice you've ever made.

She still doesn't say anything, just lifts her hand from the doorframe and steps aside. The young girl shakes her head and stomps out.

I FELL ASLEEP ON THE COUCH LAST NIGHT, WITH the balcony partway open even though the AC is always on full blast. It's the morning after the barbecue, and every morning, the same blue jay lands on my balcony and lets out a calling I can hear from my bedroom, whether the balcony door is open or not.

Right on cue, there it is, jerking its little head back and forth, hopping along the edge till it takes off again into the sky. It doesn't make any sound this time, and watching it fly away makes me wish I could jump on its back and fly away with it.

A loud knock at the door snaps me out of my daydream. It's barely nine o'clock; too early for those Seventh-day Adventist people. Jes or Derrick aren't coming over this early. Maybe it's my dad, but he wouldn't just show up without at least sending me a message.

I hear the knocks at the door again and force myself up. When I look through the peephole, I'm convinced I must still be sleeping because there's no way the person on the other side of the door is real. But when I unlock the door and

143

swing it open, there she is, standing with her back arched in a white pantsuit that is far too fancy for a house visit.

"Lady?" I say it like I don't remember who she is. So many questions are running through my head right now, like how did she know where I live, why is she here, and why so early?

"Are you going to invite me in or leave me standing out here like a stranger?"

I step aside so Lady can walk past me, and I can see her immediately start scanning my place for a critique I'm sure I'll hear about at some point. My ashtray with two roaches, the few dishes still in the sink, blanket on the couch from last night; all of these are offenses Lady can't be quiet about. I'm already bracing myself.

"What are you doing here?"

I'm not sure how that sounded coming out of my mouth. I was going for genuine curiosity but might have given "I don't want you here" vibes.

"Hello, Coi. Nice to see you, too."

Lady's back is facing me when she says this. She's standing by the balcony with her sandals still on.

"Is it really, though? Because yesterday didn't feel that nice."

Lady takes her time to turn around. She's still eyeing my apartment like she's some kind of inspector, but it's too early for me to care if she thinks I'm a slob.

"Ah, yes. Yesterday." She pauses and I'm waiting for what she has to say next. I should probably tell her to sit down but I don't want her getting too comfortable. Right now, it feels like a standoff. Like one of those old western movies minus the guns, although Lady's tongue is pretty deadly so I'm not counting violence out of the question.

"Yesterday was yesterday. I'm here now. Do you have a problem with that?"

Everything Lady says feels like a test and I don't know any of the answers. I'm thinking of what to say that will get her out of here the fastest.

"I don't even know why you're here. Yesterday might be yesterday for you, but it's not just that for me."

I hope that sounded as rude as I wanted it to. Every second Lady's here makes me remember more clearly the way she treated me at the hospital and then at the barbecue. I really don't want her at my place.

"Don't worry, I won't be long. Can we sit?"

Sitting is the opposite of not being long, but I grab my blanket off the couch and motion for Lady to have a seat.

"Are those clothes your designs?" Lady's gaze is in the direction of a clothing rack with a mashup of half-sewn tops and different shades of jean jackets with hand-painted designs on sleeves and pockets.

"Yeah, I'm working on my first real collection. Still not ready yet though."

"I used to love fashion when I was a little girl. Still do. My mother dress me up in flower dresses and these puff skirts anytime we left the house. I was like her little doll."

Pretending to smile would take up too much energy right now, so I nod in agreement even though there's nothing for me to agree with.

"I remember when I was ten and my mother gave me this gold necklace. Simple little thing with my initials on it. CD. I wore that damn necklace everywhere I went. Never took it off."

145

I've been calling my grandmother Lady so long that I almost forgot her real name is Cassandra.

"Wait, that was your necklace? The one my mom gave to me before she ripped it off my neck?"

"Yes, it was mine. And before that, it was my mother's, and then her mother's before that."

I reach for my neck knowing nothing's there, trying my best to block out the memory that's forcing its way to the surface.

"When I gave it to your mother, I told her to pass it on to her first daughter. That's the tradition. That's what connects us women together for generations. And when you disappeared for years, that tradition was being broken."

Finally, her first jab. Not like I wasn't ready for it as soon as I saw her through my peephole. I'm actually surprised it took this long.

"You realize that I didn't disappear, right? That my mom threw me out of her house. Actually, she walked me out and pretty much forgot I existed."

"And you forgot she existed. You forgot you had a mother that wasn't perfect, but she loved you."

"Wasn't perfect? She loved me?" Sitting down isn't working anymore. "Do you hear yourself, Lady? Like seriously, do you live in some kind of simulation? Because you already know what my mom did to me. You know what she was like. I'm not gonna explain this to you every time you tell me I should've turned the other cheek. You don't know what it's like to hate someone you wanna love so bad."

I'm trying my best to take breaths in between each sentence. My chest is starting to tighten, and even though I really don't want to, I sit back down, on the floor this time, and pick up the glass of water that's been on the coffee table since last night.

"Yuh calm down now?" Lady says in the same monotone voice she always uses. "You know, sometimes your mother would get into these moods where she went days and never talk to nobody. Just sit down in her room and don't come out. I know once she got into that mood, trouble coming soon after."

Who knew my mom could stay quiet for that long? From what I remember, she couldn't even stay quiet through an episode of *Housewives*.

"I tried putting her in therapy but my insurance only covered a few sessions. We tried special schools, but your mother was just too much. She fought the other kids, cussed the teachers." Lady laughs like she's remembering a specific memory. "Nothing worked. And your aunty was so young then. She was just watching your mom come home all time a night and talk to me any way she wanted to and even get violent sometimes. I had to make a choice: lose one daughter or lose two. So on her sixteenth birthday, I asked your mother to leave my house."

"You asked her to leave? Like, you gave her a choice?"

"Yes, I did give her a choice. It was behave or leave. And I still remember the day it happened."

Lady told me that my mom was in her room in one of those moods. She was already suspended from school when she and Aunty got into a fight and my mom pulled out a knife on her.

"Your aunty was only thirteen years old. Can you imagine your sister pulling out a knife on you when you're just thirteen.

When I came to see what all the commotion about, your aunt was sobbing. She was crouched down on the floor with your mother bearing over her holding that knife."

"And what did you do?"

"What you mean what did I do? I screamed for Crissy to stop and tried taking the knife from her. She turned around and looked at me with the knife still in her hand. I knew what she was thinking. I knew what she wanted to do. So even when she dropped the knife and walked to her room, I knew she had to go."

"And then you followed her to her room and watched her pack up her stuff."

"Yes. And she told me that she wasn't coming back this time. That this was the last time I would kick her out of my house."

"That's when she met my dad."

"Yes, she was staying with a friend that ended up knowing your father. And then she had you about a year later. I barely spoke to her that whole time. She didn't answer any of my calls. She only called me when she got pregnant."

I spot the blue jay back on my balcony. It's more still this time, perched on the ledge with its head in the direction of my living room. It's almost like it forgot something. Either that or it's here to check up on me.

"Why are you telling me all this?"

"Because you think you know your mother but you don't. You have no idea who she was. All you know is what you say she did to you."

"It's not what I say she did to me, it's what she did do to me. And nothing I find out about my mom is gonna change what she did. Nothing."

The blue jay is gone again and Lady makes her way to the door.

"Speak to your father," she says. "If he's such a good person, he should be telling you the truth about your mother and him relationship." Lady lingers at the doorway. "And if you're going to be part of this family, Coi, then be part of it. You're my grandchild, but I'm not a fool. I only have so much patience and you're wearing it thin. And know this: no matter how hard you fight it or how much you don't like me, that doesn't change the reality that some of my blood is running through your veins. Remember that."

MY HEADPHONES ARE ON AND I'M HOURS INTO sketching designs for my clothing line that I promised myself months ago I would drop. Lady showing up earlier almost ruined my entire day, but I got this burst of energy and all I want to do is design.

I know I don't remember much from the fashion show that Derrick and I went to, but I do remember the vibe. So many people showed up and were genuinely excited to sit and watch and take pictures of clothing from a local designer that no one outside of that room had ever heard of. That should be me.

It will be me.

It has to be me.

The few pieces I put up on IG earlier this year were designs I started when I was still in high school. The idea I have for Coy Kids is so much deeper than that. I'm speaking to someone. To that young girl who laughs at jokes she doesn't think is funny. To the young boy who plays video games with his friends when he rather be reading graphic novels. Coy Kids is like a members-only club that you don't need an invite to. You don't even need to be a kid. You just have to feel that youthful curiosity, that unexplainable energy that doesn't come from being loud but comes from being exactly who you are. This is for my generation. At least that's what I'm going for.

And these sketches are the closest to what's been in my mind. I can't wait to show Jes. She's been pushing me to get these sketches done since I told her about the concept, a concept I've been sort of playing with since I went to fashion camp a few years ago. That was a two-week boot camp on the campus of Stanford University in California. Before that camp, I was interested in fashion but still heavy into art. When I left, all I could think about was starting my first line. That's when I told my dad about this whole fashion thing.

I'm so lucky that I can zone out to all of this stuff. That I can lose myself in shapes and silhouettes while all it would take for my world to crumble is one brick being pulled from this shaky foundation. Maybe my world has always been this fragile. Maybe. But since Aunty sent me that message about my mom being in the hospital, I've struggled to contain the flood that's pushing against my walls, and now there are cracks and water is leaking out and I don't know which hole to plug first.

Except that I do. And when I finally put my sketches away, I grab my phone and text Kayla. When a minute goes by and she doesn't answer, I call her. Three rings and I don't really expect her to answer, but when she says hello like I'm a bad ex-boyfriend she's trying to get over, I'm relieved.

"Hey little sis." I don't even know why I just said that. And when Kayla doesn't say anything back, I drop the act.

"Listen, I'm sorry. For a lot of things, but . . . can we meet up? I mean, do you wanna meet up? You can come by my place. I have my own apartment now. Not sure if you knew that. But, yeah, you should come by. I can Uber you over. What do you think?"

Silence is a strange thing. It's literally nothing, but you can hear it. You feel it, how uncomfortable it is.

"You there, sis?"

"You want me to come right now?"

"Yeah, why not? I don't have anything to do for the rest of the day. We can order food or whatever. Whatever you wanna do."

———

Kayla's Uber is two minutes away and I haven't sat down since we got off the phone. I have no idea what to say to her, but that's not what's keeping me pacing around my apartment. The thing that makes me want to rip my hair out is that I don't even know what she's going through. I'm the only person who's mattered for the past few months. Me. My life. My problems. My bullshit. And now . . .

I meet Kayla downstairs just as she's stepping out of the car. She's wearing an oversized long-sleeved white shirt and baggy gray sweatpants, a look I pulled off a lot when I was about her age. She throws a backpack over one shoulder and doesn't move away from the car door.

Are we the same height now? Standing with her head slightly tilted down, Kayla looks like she's grown inches since I last saw her at the hospital. Her hair is slicked back in a high bun, and when she finally cracks half a smile it's like I'm back in my dream staring at our mother.

"You gonna stand there or come give your sister a hug?"

Kayla rests her head on my shoulder but keeps her arms straight. I wrap both my arms around her and kiss her cheek.

"You good?" I ask, and she just looks at me with that half smile still on her face.

Upstairs, Kayla's eyes open a little wider .

"This is yours?"

"For now, yeah. I'm renting it."

"But you live here by yourself?"

"Just me."

Kayla throws her knapsack to the floor and runs straight to the balcony.

"You can see the lake from here. And that's the CN Tower over there."

I watch Kayla lean over the balcony and take in the entire view. That's the same way I reacted when Derrick's mom showed it to me, so I know what Kayla's going through. I make a mental note to spend more time on my balcony, especially on rainy days when I can't go for walks.

"I can't wait to get my own place," Kayla says, "away from everybody. Just me on my own."

We're both on the balcony now, sitting on lawn chairs I bought from a yard sale just a couple weeks ago.

"Is that what you want? To be on your own?"

"I'm already on my own. I just wanna make it official. Like, I wish everyone would just leave me alone so I can do whatever I wanna do."

I feel like my therapist. She would've heard me say something like that and not even blinked. But I'm not my therapist. Hearing my sister say she's already alone when she lives at home with her father and is supposed to have an older sister makes it hard for me not to rush out of this chair and wrap my arms around her like I did when we were kids.

I think about telling Kayla that everyone is here for her, but if there's one thing I learned from my therapist is that listening is more effective than talking.

"Everyone at school kept asking me questions. Asking me stuff about my mom or whatever. Or asking me how I felt. Even the teachers."

"Is that why you didn't wanna go back?"

"I didn't wanna go back because Mom died. She was gone. And our house was quiet, and Daddy never says anything about Mom. He acts like it never happened."

Kayla tells me that she ran away. Not exactly ran away, but "didn't go home" is how she put it. After school one day, she went to the mall, then went to the movie theater and watched one movie and snuck into the other. By the time the movies were done, it was after ten o'clock. When she finally walked back into her house, Dave had already called the police.

"Daddy was so mad," Kayla says. "But I didn't care. I didn't wanna be in that house. It was too . . . quiet."

Kayla also tells me about getting into her first fight at school and then getting sent to the office for saying something nasty to the teacher. When I ask her what she said, she doesn't want to repeat it.

We stay on the balcony till the sun starts to set, till the sky turns colors that feel like psychedelics, and I realize that I've never spoken to my sister like this. Not this version of her, not in this kind of depth. When we finally head back inside, it's like I know who she is now. I understand her, not just as my sister but as a young girl dealing with some heavy shit. Every question I asked or any prompt I gave was like turning the pages in a book about her life. A book I should've read already.

I sit down in my single-seater and Kayla lays down on the couch.

"Why didn't you come to Mom's funeral?"

I know this is one of the questions I have to deal with. I know it's been at the front of Kayla's mind since I met her downstairs and now she's finally comfortable enough to confront her big sister. But I've brushed this question off so many times before — not from anyone else, but from myself. I've tried my best to avoid what not going to my mom's funeral really means, and that meaning changes depending on if I just spoke to Jes or had a convo with Derrick, or if I smoked a joint or am alone for hours with no client work to do and a mind that's like skydiving without a parachute.

"Why don't you come stay with me?" I'm thinking about it as the words leave my mouth.

"You didn't answer my question."

"Just for the summer."

Kayla keeps looking at me, not saying a word. I take a breath. "Listen, I don't know how to answer that question. There's a lot of stuff I'm still trying to figure out. But I know how you feel, Kayla. I know what you're going through right now. Before you do something drastic that you're gonna regret, give me a chance to make you not feel so alone." I switch seats and sit playfully on Kayla's legs. "Please, please, please, please, please, come stay with me."

Kayla's face softens, but then she sits up and looks me straight in the eyes for the first time since she got here.

"Almost six months. Almost six months since Mom died and since you talked to me."

I hate myself.

That's my first thought. It's the thought that replays over and over and over while I try to keep my sister's gaze. What can I say? What excuse can I make up to explain 180 days of absence, of silence, of selfishness? I see the tears building up in Kayla's eyes and feel my own ready to flow.

"Do you hate our family that much?"

Wiping the tears from Kayla's face, I think about looking back at her the day my mom walked me out. Her stare was naive then, not frightened or angry or sad or knowing, just curious about why her sister was leaving, the same way she would be if I left to go to the convenience store without telling her. She had no way to know that I wasn't coming back. But right now, sitting next to me, that same naivete has been replaced with anger and fear and sadness, and her curiosity replaced by years of confusion about who I am. Me. Her older sister who hasn't been a sister since I looked back.

Every answer to her question flashing through my brain feels hypocritical.

Do I hate our family? No, no I don't. I love Aunty and like Dave, and, okay, maybe I hate Lady. And my mother. My mother. Do I hate you? Do I still hate you?

156

"I don't hate our family, Kayla. And I love you. You're my sister. And I'm sorry I haven't been there but that's gonna change. I promise it will."

Our cheeks are pressed tightly enough together for us to squish each other's tears.

"Daddy will never say yes."

We finally peel away from each other.

"You let me worry about your dad. You just let me know what you wanna do and I'll take care of the rest."

"I THINK YOU'RE CRAZY." DERRICK IS STANDING IN between my couch and the balcony. "How is making your sister stay with you gonna make things better?"

"I don't know," I say. I'm filing my nails with Griselda playing low in the background. "It just feels right."

"It just feels right? You're not even making any sense."

"Does it have to make sense for it to be right?"

I'm not even looking at Derrick and I know he rolled his eyes. He came over last night after my sister left. I told him about my idea this morning, and he hasn't been able to shut up about it.

"And you think your stepdad and grandmother are gonna just hand Kayla over because they like you so much and think you're a great role model?"

"I don't know, D, I'm just rolling with this right now. Maybe they will, maybe they won't. But I know I can help Kayla. And I told you a million times already that it's just for the rest of the summer. I'll be outta this apartment by then, but Kayla needs this right now."

I turn up the volume on the speakers from my phone, walk into my bathroom and shut the door. Derrick hates when I end our conversations like that, but I can't keep saying the same thing over and over again. He doesn't think I can handle this; I get it. But I can. I have to. And there's another reason I came into the bathroom. There's a missed call on my phone from Lady, and she left a voice message. I don't want to check it in front of Derrick because I already know what I'm about to hear, and I don't want Lady's negativity fueling Derrick's energy.

"Yuh head nuh good?" That's the first statement from Lady as I sit on the toilet with the lid down. Her patois sounds threatening over the phone, every sentence an accusation or an insult. *"You tink you alone cyan mine Kayla? Me rather dead then send my grand-pickney fi stay wit yuh."*

I get to the end of the message and play it again, picturing Lady screaming through speakerphone before calling me two more times. It doesn't matter that I won't pick up. The torment of me seeing her number and knowing what she has to say is more than enough satisfaction for her. One more unanswered call and her job is done.

"Whatever, Coi," Derrick yells from outside of the bathroom door. "This is stupid. I'm outta here."

I listen to Lady's message one more time then get out of the bathroom. I know she might be right, so might Derrick, but I don't care. I don't. But when I get a text from Dave saying *call me*, I get the same feeling I do when I'm about to post a new drop on IG, except the stakes are so much higher than whether or not people like or buy my designs.

My place suddenly feels too small for this conversation, so I step out on my balcony to call him.

"Take her." Dave's words are so sudden that I don't think he's talking to me.

"Take her?"

"Yes, take her. She needs it. She needs some space."

"And you trust me?" Those words leave my mouth as soon as they enter my mind.

"I trust you, Coi. And Kayla loves you. No matter what happened, she loves you, for real."

Before I can say thank you, Kayla's texting me rows of smiley emojis.

"Only thing we need to do is convince your grandmother."

"Any ideas on that one? Because she already called me cussing on my voice mail."

"Yeah, Kayla got excited and spilled the beans. But let me worry about that. At the end of the day, I'm Kayla's father so I make the final decision."

I'M NOT SURE WHAT DAVE DID OR SAID TO LADY, BUT the next day, Kayla's at my door first thing in the morning. On our first full day together, we're wearing robes with cotton between our toes and pulling masks off our faces. I pulled my braids out last night and now conditioner is sitting in both of our hair, wrapped and drying in white towels. Kayla raps along to the Rico Nasty songs and bops her head to 21 Savage. I ask her who her favorite rapper is and she shrugs her shoulders.

Halfway through the third episode of *Bridgerton* we've watched in a row, Kayla asks if I have a ring light.

"For what? You wanna post some videos?"

"No. Ummm . . . can I . . ."

It's not hard for me to remember what it was like being fourteen. Living without my mom was still new to me, and even though my dad's footprints were always right beside mine, I still questioned every step that I took or decision that I made.

"Just say it, sis. Whatever you want, just say it."

Kayla will have to figure out a lot of stuff on her own. She'll have to learn to not blame herself, to trust herself, to not be overcome by the bad days, the days that waves of loneliness crash whatever mood she's in and barely let up before they crash in again.

"Can I do your makeup?"

"My makeup? You wanna do my makeup?" Whatever I was expecting to hear, it wasn't this.

"Never mind. I'll probably mess it up, anyway."

"No, no. It's fine. I just didn't know you can do makeup. I don't even think I've ever seen you wear makeup."

"Mom wouldn't let me leave the house with makeup on, but I did it all the time."

Why am I so surprised right now? We grew up watching our mom do other people's hair at least once or twice a week. Plus Kayla was old enough to remember me drawing and coloring scenes from my imagination. Mom didn't let us hang anything on the walls, so I kept those drawings in a wide shoebox Dave lent me that I put under my bed.

"Okay, let's do it. Let me grab some from my room."

We set up in the living room — foundation, mascara, bronzer, blush, eyeliner, lipstick spread across the floor. Kayla sits me down on a chair, picks up a brush and gets to work. She takes her time checking each section she covers, her eyebrows forced close together when she steps back to view what she's done.

Kayla mumbles to herself when she thinks something's off but doesn't say anything else unless I ask her.

"How long have you known how to do this?"

"Since I was like ten."

"Ten? For real? How did you learn?"

"Mom let me practice on her. I'd watch YouTube videos

on my iPad then try it out on myself. Mom always took pictures of me before we wiped it off my face. Then one day she told me to try doing her makeup."

Kayla's tracing eyeliner around my lids as she speaks.

"Mom let you do that?"

"Yeah. The first few times we did it, she rubbed it off right after. Then one day she kept it on, and whenever she was going out, she'd call me into her room and have all the makeup ready on the bed. When I finished, she'd pose in the mirror, kiss me on my forehead and say 'my little girl.'"

I tried. I tried thinking back to any moment that me and my mother shared that felt so intimate. Even a kiss on the forehead would've been something. Anything. But no memory I can recall made me feel like a daughter to a mother that gave a shit.

Kayla hands me the mirror and hovers over me as I scope my face.

"It's perfect." And it is. I look like I'm ready to star in a L'Oréal commercial. Kayla pretends to flip her hair back and snaps her fingers. I'm still looking in the mirror in awe of how good my makeup looks. "I had no idea you could do this, sis."

"There's a lot you don't know about me," she says, and it stings, even though I'm not sure Kayla said it with any kind of animosity.

"You're right, so why don't you tell me?"

Kayla laughs, and now there's no mistaking the sarcasm.

"You mean the four years you disappeared or just the last few months?"

I deserve that.

163

"Four and a half, actually. Why don't you start by telling me where you go at night?"

"Oh, I guess my dad told you. What else did he tell you?"

"A lot. When I asked him about you staying with me, he told me some of the problems you two are going through. But he said what scares him most is when you don't come home till late at night. He says you don't answer your phone or let him know where you are. You're fourteen, Kayla. You haven't even started high school yet. And even if you had, you shouldn't be outside by yourself late at night."

Kayla hitches herself to the corner of the couch.

"There's a lot of things that shouldn't be happening, but they do."

"Kayla, where do you go?"

Kayla folds her arms and turns away from me, and it's like I can feel the force of the shield she's put around herself.

"Do you even miss Mom?" she asks. "Like, do you ever think about her or wish she was still here?"

It was so much easier to look at myself in the mirror a minute ago. To see my reflection and feel proud. Kayla's question makes me see the mirror cracking the longer I look, till it's split into hundreds of shards that deform my reflection to someone unrecognizable.

I do miss Mom. I missed her for years, until I didn't. Or couldn't. Or tried not to.

Each of these thoughts feels like an injection. Like a needle slowly penetrating my skull before it finds another spot, another thought.

"My relationship with Mom was different than yours. You know that."

164

"But she was still our mom and . . ."

"She was still *your* mom, not mine. She wasn't there for me, Kayla. I don't know what happened when I left. Maybe she changed. Maybe. But she went years without me in her life. She wasn't my mother."

Kayla wipes a tear before it trickles down her face.

"How can you say that?"

How *can* I say that? Maybe she wasn't a good mother to me, but she was still my mother. That means something. It should mean something. But I can't explain to Kayla what that thing is because I don't know. What I can do is sit beside her, open my arms and let her fall as far as she needs to, knowing that I'll be there to brace the impact. Because no matter what, it's going to hurt.

"I go to Mom's grave," Kayla says. "When I'm out at night, that's where I am. It's so scary walking through there by myself in the dark but I do it. And I'm still scared when I get to Mom's grave, but . . . I don't know. I just . . . do you think I'm crazy?"

"No, of course not. You're not crazy at all."

"I feel like it. And every day feels the same."

What's really crazy is that I can see Kayla still falling and I wonder how long she's been hoping for someone to catch her. Or maybe that's the problem. Maybe she's lost hope.

"SO KAYLA IS STAYING WITH YOU NOW." IT frustrates me how soothing my mom's voice is in this world. She speaks much slower than she did in real life, and her pronouncing every syllable of every word almost demands that I listen to what she has to say.

"How do you know that? Are you watching me? Or watching over me? Because it would've meant a lot more if you did this when you weren't some kind of figment of my imagination."

"Hostile already?"

"Yes. Yes, I am hostile. Why is this happening? All of this. Why am I seeing you in my dreams? You're dead, and before you were dead you were dead to me. So I don't know why I'm dealing with all this. I don't want to deal with all of this."

The same way all my other dreams start, it's just me and my mom alone in a blank space. There's a distance between us that I'm covering while I spew all the anger I can at her.

"I should be thinking about fashion and my boyfriend who probably hates me and spending time with my friends.

But I'm here being haunted when I've already suffered in real life. It's bullshit."

I can't tell if I'm getting closer to my mom or not. She hasn't moved and I'm stomping furiously toward her.

"Coi."

Scream.

Cuss.

Tell me I'm worthless.

Make me hate you again. Anything but this.

"Take my hand."

I'm close enough now to touch my mom's outstretched palm. Even in the midst of my venting, I grab her hand without a second thought.

"Give me your other hand, too."

I'm so mad I can feel my body vibrate. I can feel my heart trying to burst out of my chest and all my muscles tighten.

"I hate this!"

"Tell me what you hate, Coi."

"This, I hate all of it."

"Coi, look at me. Tell me what you hate."

I squeeze my mom's hands as tight as I can and scream as loud as I can till I fall on my knees. My mom crouches down with me, our hands still in each other's.

"Tell me what you hate."

I WAKE UP ON MY COUCH UNCOVERED. I'M STILL IN my robe and house socks but minus the towel covering my head. It's dark outside, which means it can't be morning yet, and when I take a peek into my room, I see Kayla wrapped under the blankets. I should probably go back to sleep till the sun makes an appearance, but I remember my photography professor telling the class that you should never have to force yourself to sleep. If you're awake, be awake.

I decide to try out a new hot chocolate bundle I bought at a store in the Distillery District. I put a small pot of milk to boil and wait near the balcony, where light from groups of tall and short buildings bring the lake to life. I can see my jogging trail from here, from the leaf-covered entrance to the park that I stop at before turning around and walking back home. The four kilometers doesn't look as long as the twenty-two minutes (on a good day) it takes me to finish, and even though I can't make it out in the dark, I picture the spot on my walk back where I sit on the rocks close enough to the lake for me to feed the swans.

Seeing the swans close up is my favorite part of this routine. They glide tall across the water with perfect posture, their white feathers pristine like they've been untouched by nature. Sometimes I catch a group of two or three baby swans floating with their mother. The first time I saw this scene, they floated right up to the rocks. That's when I first noticed that the mother's eyes were red. A strange kind of red. Not quite dark but not quite bright, but when you see them, it completely transforms the way you interpret the swan's behavior. They're not gliding across the water as much as they're patrolling. The gild of their white feathers appears more like a uniform than a coat. I've never had a negative encounter with a swan, but I instinctively know that they are not to be played with.

The milk in the pot is almost at a boil, so I throw in a stick of chocolate and stir. It's quiet enough for me to hear the mixture sway against the wooden ladle. A few minutes and the chocolate is blended. I take a small spoon and taste, mix for another minute then pour half a glass into a small teacup.

One day. It's only been one full day and I already feel like I need to recharge. That's a good thing though, right? I should feel like I expended some energy, lots of energy. I have lots of making up to do. Or I should say that I have a lot of time to make up for. Whatever. I'm doing what I need to do, what I feel like doing.

Sitting with one foot up on my single-seater blowing steam from the top of my mug, my mom's words come back to me.

Tell me what you hate.

That was my chance. I could've let her have it. I could've told her exactly how those five years made me feel about her. She was asking for it. She was asking for it and all I could do was fall to my knees and cry.

Would it have been different in real life? These aren't just dreams I'm having anymore, so how much more real do I need it to be?

Tell me what you hate.

Why didn't she say "who"? Was she referring to something specific that I'm missing? Something I can't see? Because it should be who. It should be her. What else could it be?

You're overthinking this, Coi.

I don't know if that's my voice I'm hearing or my mother's. Both are tangled and I haven't been awake long enough to unravel what last night's dream means. I know that I was angry. Angrier than I've been in any other dream. I'm still releasing some of those emotions with every sip of this hot chocolate, but that tension is hard to shake. And I don't even know if I want to shake it. I should be angry. I should stay angry. That's what she deserves.

Wow, I sound so stupid. *"That's what she deserves."* She's gone. My mother is gone and never coming back. And I should let go of whatever I'm holding on to, but I can't figure out why. Why should I let go? Does her dying make everything okay? Every belt to the back, every time I had to miss school to take care of my sister in the mornings because she was too tired from doing nothing to wake up. Every insult, every criticism, every terrible thing she told me about my father, what am I supposed to do with that?

Let it go.

Is that my voice or hers? Maybe it doesn't matter. I've been holding on to this for so long that it's given me anxiety, forced me into therapy, made me believe it was okay to skip her funeral. What benefit have I gained from holding on?

"Hey." Kayla's voice sounds angelic cutting through the quiet chaos in my head. "What are you doing awake?"

"Drinking hot chocolate. Want some?" I pour the rest of the chocolate from the pot into a mug and Kayla and I stay standing in the kitchen.

"This tastes weird."

"That's what hot chocolate is really supposed to taste like. It's real chocolate, not that stuff you buy from No Frills."

"I'll stick to No Frills."

Every time Kayla laughs or smiles, I count it as a point. There are going to be so many times I'll have to remind her to be happy, so cataloging these smiles now is like insurance.

"It's still really early," I say. "You should go back to bed."

Kayla puts down her cup and holds out both her hands.

"Come with me. Sleeping in your room alone is scary."

I'm not sure if Kayla is joking or not, but I put my teacup down and let her take my hands.

"I hope you don't snore," I say.

One more point.

"NUTELLA SMOOTHIE WITH A LITTLE BIT OF HONEY?" My dad hasn't stopped grinning since I walked in the door. We're a short streetcar ride away from each other, but this is only the second or third time I've visited since I moved out. Kayla's at my hairdresser getting knotless braids. We have plans later and I told her I'd meet up with her after I leave here.

We cheers with Nutella smoothies and my dad launches into the big news he had to tell me in person.

"I signed a publishing deal."

"Dad! Really? That's amazing."

"I know. I've been working on this book and trying to get it published forever, so when my agent called me last week to say an official offer came in, I almost lost it."

My dad's shaking his head in disbelief. It's been years since he started this novel and even longer since he's been talking about it.

"Next step, bestseller!"

"You know it!" Dad and I slap hands and that grin gets wider. "I can't believe this is actually happening. It feels like a dream."

My dad doesn't jump when we watch scary movies, and his favorite thing to say to me when I got a high grade or when something happens with my fashion is "good job," so to see him this expressive lets me know how much this means to him.

"So what about you, my daughter? What have you been up to?"

"Not much. Except that Kayla lives with me now."

"What? Kayla's living with you?"

"Just for as long as I'm at the apartment. It's a long story."

I tell my dad about what was happening with Kayla and how I lost it at the barbecue.

"It just made sense, you know? I wanted to be there for her because I've been in my own world for so long."

"I get it, and I know that despite everything you have a big heart, Coi. But are you sure you're gonna be able to deal with someone else's emotions and energy when you still haven't figured out yours?"

It's a question I would've got defensive about if Kayla hadn't been living with me for two weeks already. But now I know the type of effort and energy it takes to make sure that she's good, so I understand where my dad's coming from.

"I probably wasn't ready, to be real. But I'm so glad I'm doing it because we're actually building a relationship now. It's like I'm meeting this whole new person who I've known my entire life."

None of what I said is easing the concerned expression on Dad's face. Even though he's nodding in agreement, he's gnawing on the inside of his lip.

"I'm good, Dad, I can handle it. Don't worry about me. You got a book coming out that needs to sell a million copies.

We should be celebrating, and not with Nutella smoothies."

That did it. Dad dips into the refrigerator and pulls out a bottle of champagne.

"You ever pop one of these things?" he asks.

"Nope, never."

"Well there's a first time for everything."

He hands me the bottle and walks me through how to pop the cork. I pour both of us a glass and we stand and cheers again.

"To dreams coming true," I say.

"To dreams coming true."

Dad takes a gulp and I settle for a small sip. I actually don't like champagne, which is why I've never popped a bottle.

"Speaking of dreams," Dad says, "are you still having those strange dreams about your mother?"

I haven't had one since the first night Kayla slept over, but I don't really want to go over it with him. "Once in a while. But there's something else I wanna ask you about."

"Go for it."

"Lady popped up at my place the other day. Like before Kayla moved in. She told me I should talk to you about my mom."

My dad takes another sip of champagne and rests his glass on the kitchen counter.

"Okay . . . was there anything specific that you wanna know?"

"I don't know. I mean, Lady told me this whole story about my mom pulling out a knife on Aunty and that's why she kicked her out. I guess she wants me to see a different side of my mom or something. Or try to explain why my

174

mom is the way she is, or was the way she was, I should say."

My dad walks over to the corner where there are two barstools and a high table and I follow him.

"Everybody has more than one side to them. Your mom was no different. And yeah, that story Lady told you is true, but it's so much deeper than that."

"There's a deeper reason for my mom threatening Aunty's life?"

"I'm saying that it's easy to look at what she did in the moment as crazy or whatever, but unless you know the full picture, then you can't really judge."

My dad has always been careful about how he speaks to me about my mom. He made sure not to say anything negative about her when I was around. When he first got full custody, he'd ask me if I wanted to call her or go visit my sister. He didn't know I already accepted never seeing my mom again and that my mom had made up her mind that I wasn't part of her family as soon as my dad reversed out of that driveway.

But this conversation feels different. It doesn't feel like my dad is trying to protect me from something; it almost feels like he's hiding something.

"What aren't you telling me?" My dad has been squeezing his knuckles together the whole time. "Dad, we've already been through the worst. Nothing you say is gonna change anything between us."

I wonder how many lies parents tell their kids in the name of "protecting" us. I don't need to be inside my dad's head to know that he's weighing his options. How much? How little? Which details should he leave out?

"You must've been like five or six months old," my dad starts. "We were still living in Elaine's basement, of course, when your mom comes walking down the steps with you in one arm. I wasn't really paying much attention until I heard other footsteps trailing behind her."

I have no idea where this story is going, but I reach to the side of the high table and open a box of water.

"I don't really know who it is or what's going on until both of them stand directly in between me and the TV. Then I literally jump to my feet."

"Who was it?"

My dad takes a long gulp of champagne.

"Funny, that's almost the same question your mom asked. She pointed at the girl standing beside her and asked me if I knew who this was. And I did know who it was but I couldn't say anything. I just stood there biting my lip."

My dad's building the suspense like it's one of his books when I really just want him to get to the point.

"Then she changed up her tone and asked me *how* I knew the girl standing beside her. And I say something stupid like 'I don't know' or 'I forget.' I don't exactly remember, I just know it was dumb. And then your mom turns to the girl and asks how she knows me and . . ."

"And?"

"Listen, Coi, the reason I never told you this before is because I'm not that person anymore. But . . . I cheated on Crissy. More than once with that girl while you were still just a baby."

"You cheated?"

"Yeah, I did."

"You? My father who I thought was the only good person left on this earth. You cheated?"

"More than once."

"Why? Wait, let me guess. You were young, right? Just a kid? Didn't know what you were doing?"

Dad rubs his hands over his face like he's trying to wipe it clean.

"I can give you a bunch of reasons. And yes, I was still a teenager. And yes, your mom was my first real relationship and I didn't know how to handle all that responsibility, never mind being a father. And those are probably good excuses, but it's all bullshit. I just did it because I felt like it, and when you're immature, it's hard to understand that you need to put loyalty and responsibility ahead of your emotions sometimes."

"But she had your child, Dad. She had me. How could you . . ."

I'm looking at the same father who carried me to bed on his back every night. The same father who made snow angels with me even though he didn't have any snow pants. This is the same father who took my hand when my mother let me go and gave me life, gave me a purpose, gave me a reason.

"So that's why Mom hated you. She could never get over that, could she?"

"It was hard for her. We were each other's first love. We spent every day together for months, and that started before she got pregnant. But we were kids. We thought we'd be together forever but we were just kids."

That's always the excuse, isn't it? We were young. We didn't know what we were doing. We were just kids. And it's like we're supposed to remove the scarlet letter from young people as they grow up, no matter how many lives they mess up. Because forgiveness is real and everyone deserves some form of retribution, right? Where would we be if we didn't turn the other cheek?

"And that's why my mom hated me, too, right? I always reminded her of you. I always took your side. I loved you more even though you did her wrong."

"Crissy didn't hate you, Coi. She . . ."

"It doesn't matter. It doesn't matter what you think. I never felt love in that home. I never felt anything except my mom's rage."

"It was a long time ago, Coi. Your mother and I both did things to each other that we're not proud of. I did everything I could to be a better person and a good father, but you're right; she never got past it. She always held it against me."

"You mean she always held it against *me*. Me! I'm the one who suffered. I'm the one she looked at every day and saw your fuck-up."

I'm trying right now. I'm really trying to remember who I'm talking to. My dad's waiting for me to say something else but there's nothing left. He did what he did and nothing's going to change that, except that I had to endure whatever part of him my mother saw in me. I was blessed and cursed with the same blood.

"I gotta get outta here," I say. "Me and Kayla are headed out soon."

I shuffle past my dad, who doesn't say anything. He watches me step into my shoes and walk out the door.

August

I CAN HEAR ELAINE'S WORDS LIKE SHE'S SPEAKING them directly into my ear. "Be careful what you tell yourself." For the last few weeks, I've been telling myself that my dad is the one to blame. That because he couldn't control his teenage hormones, my mother took out her hate for him on me. That I've been tortured for all these years because of him.

Be careful what you tell yourself.

I've been ignoring my dad's calls since that conversation. He sends me texts I don't answer and I'm just waiting for him to show up at my apartment. Today I had to remind myself that this is my father. The father who was my only parent for the last five years. The same father who raised a daughter through her teenage years and is still alive to tell about it. He's the reason I know what love feels like. Why am I telling myself anything different?

Hey. I add a peace sign and heart emoji to the text. Dad sends back the emoji with one tear coming down its face.

I'm sorry. I don't hate you. You're literally the best dad in the world. I'm on the couch with my feet up on the coffee table.

Kayla's in the bathroom finishing up a shower. *I'm having my first fashion show next week. You gotta be there.*

I'm there. Send me deets.

No one says deets dad. See you next week!

"You getting nervous yet?"

Kayla is out of the shower in a new pink robe I bought her.

"I been nervous since I set the date."

"You mean since Jes set the date?"

Kayla is getting pro at taking jabs.

"Hey, we all need a little push sometimes."

A little push is an understatement. After I told Jes that I didn't think I'd have any designs ready for the summer, she took my phone and posted that my first fashion show would be on August 15th. She added a pic of one of the designs that was in my phone, then told me, "Guess you'll need to get moving."

I wanted to rip her head off for like a day, but then I realized that the designs I was already working on were actually pretty good. No, they were really good. So I kept working. Every day, I'd get my client work done early and then spend the rest of the day creating new designs. Kayla was my muse. I'd put her in different outfits to see what they looked like. She even gave me some suggestions on designs, which I listened to because Kayla is the type of girl I see wearing this collection.

Kayla also started recording me cutting and sewing and screaming when things didn't go right. I'd post those clips on my TikTok and people loved them. Now the show is a week away and my stomach is doing backflips.

"Is your dad coming?" Kayla asks.

"Yeah, I was just texting him before you got out the shower. I'm still getting over everything but there's no way I'd want him to miss this."

"What about Lady?"

"Is that a joke? Because there's zero chance that's happening."

Kayla doesn't say anything. She walks into the bedroom and slides the door closed. I follow behind her and slide it open.

"You get why I don't want her to come, right?"

"I get it."

"But?"

"But nothing. I just know that Lady is really into fashion."

I always need to remind myself that although Kayla and I are sisters, we've lived two separate lives. We more or less grew up around the same people, but our relationships with those people aren't the same.

"Well you can send her the recording once it's over. I don't want her there."

Kayla chuckles.

"What? What's so funny?"

"If you only knew how much you sound like Mom right now."

I MIGHT THROW UP IN MY MOUTH. WE'RE ABOUT TO open the doors to my very first fashion show and I'm thinking of ways I can keep those doors closed and tell everyone waiting outside that I was just kidding when I said my line is ready.

"Too late." Jes is inside my head again. "No turning back now. You're gonna do this and it's gonna be amazing."

I have to admit that the setup in here looks stunning. When Jes first showed me the space, I knew right away how I could bring it to life. It's a dance studio and most of the walls are covered by mirrors, so I dressed mannequins I borrowed from school and posed them in front of the mirrors so it almost looks like they just got dressed.

I also wanted to show off my art. I've been painting a lot of portraits lately, with just enough distortion to make them feel abstract. All of the images are inspired by the girls and women in my life and at different points. My favorite is this group portrait that's meant to show four generations of women. They're all linking their arms together in a full circle so that the first and last of the generation are locked together. Jes says this piece is my subconscious.

Since the building is old with lots of exposed pipes along the roof, I was able to tie strings to my art and hang some of those portrait pieces. So once those doors open, people are going to be walking through what looks like a forest of floating canvases before getting to a clearing where the actual fashion show will happen.

"You ready?" Derrick's behind me rubbing my shoulders.

"Of course she's ready," Jes jumps in. "She's been ready for this her whole life, right, Coi?"

I try to show Jes an ounce of the confident girl she's accustomed to but am much more focused on not losing my breath.

"Let's do it!"

The best part about seeing all these people here is that I don't know most of them. When I sent out formal invites for the show, I thought maybe twenty people would show up, and I was fine with that. We had twenty people RSVP the first day and over a hundred and fifty people in total. So yeah, I'm kind of losing my mind. Or I should say I *was* losing my mind. Now that everyone's here and weaving through the art pieces and taking selfies in the mirror beside the mannequins, it all feels right. Like I'm supposed to be here. Like this is supposed to be happening.

It's also good to see Kayla this excited. She's standing with Aunty now, who was one of the first faces I saw when I opened the doors. Aunty's been seeing me draw and paint since I was a toddler, so she's probably feeling all kinds of proud right now. Pharaoh's not with her. Dave agreed to babysit so he's not here. My dad is, though, because he's always here for me. That's the new story I've been telling myself.

He's playing it cool. After hugging me and telling me how proud he is, he's stayed away. I'm watching him now standing close to the entrance looking down at his cell phone and I suddenly have this urge to run over to him. He catches my eye and gives me a little wave and I pretend like I'm being forced to walk over.

"You happy?" he asks, putting his phone away in his pocket.

"I think so. How can I not be, right?"

Dad pulls me in for a half hug, but when I look up at his face, it looks like he's just seen a car wreck in real time. When I follow his eyes, my face drops, too.

"Happy to see me?" Lady says.

No way. No freaking way.

Why? How? Why?

"Hi, Lady." My dad breaks the awkwardness. "I didn't know you were coming."

"That's because I wasn't invited, but I wouldn't miss my granddaughter's first show. She knows how much I love fashion."

There must be steam rising off the top of my head. She can't be here. She shouldn't be here.

"You're not going to say hi to your grandmother, Coi?" she says.

I'm not doing this with her. Not today. Not here. I don't say anything. I just slip away toward where the models will be walking soon and my dad follows behind me.

"She's doing this on purpose," I tell my dad, still in full stride. "She knows she's not here to support me. She's here to get me mad or distracted or . . . she's not here for anything good."

186

My dad grabs my arm and spins me around.

"Hey. Listen to me. This is your day. *Your* day. No one else's. You've worked hard for this, you're great at this, and you deserve to enjoy your day. Don't worry about Lady or anything else that's trying to stop you from living in this moment."

I hear everything my dad's saying and I know it's true. But when I look over his shoulder and still see Lady, I spin back around, head to the back room, and slam the door shut. All the models turn around at the sound of the door slamming and stare at me. I'm staring back at all the outfits they're wearing, outfits I've designed and am about to show a crowd of excited supporters.

"We ready?" I say that more confidently than I actually feel. The room erupts in cheers and suddenly all I can think about is how dope this show's about to be. I open the door and give a thumbs-up to the DJ. While he gathers the crowd to the runway, I do a final check on the models, adjust some accessories, and line them up. The models look like they're somewhere in between a nineties R&B girl group video and front row at a Nirvana show. They're all in vibrant-colored, oversized graphic T-shirts blended with more denim than should be allowed on a runway, but I'm loving it.

The lights dim except for a spotlight on the runway. One by one, each model struts just like we practiced. As much as I'm watching them to make sure nothing goes wrong, I'm scanning the room for reactions. I'm seeing heads turning toward each other, whispering words with smiles on their faces. I'm reading lips mouthing "I love that" when a model passes close by. Aunty and Kayla are together, watching me as much as they're watching the show. They both give me an overexuberant wave and I can't help but laugh and wave back.

When my scanning takes me over to the entrance, I spot Lady and my dad talking. I know that look on my dad's face. He's the most patient person I know, but that look means all his patience is out the window.

"Don't worry about it right now." Jes is so close to me when she says it that her lips touch my ear. "I see it, too. Not now though, Coi. Back to the show." Derrick's close, too, and he wraps his arm around me without saying a word.

I grudgingly pull my eyes away from the scene. Jes is right, though. I need to focus on this show. There are only a few more pieces left and then I can think about how to handle Lady. Plus I know my dad won't make Lady do anything to ruin this night.

When the last model walks off the runway, I walk on and take a bow like we're really at Paris Fashion Week and Anna Wintour is in the audience sitting next to Rihanna. I hear Aunty and Kayla's cheers above the applause from everyone else. I take one more bow before sliding back over to where me and Jes were standing.

"Now what?" I say.

"I think your dad can handle himself."

"I know, but it's not even about that. I should be talking to everyone who came here to see me and instead I'm worried about what she's gonna say or do. It's just her energy that worries me."

Before Jes has a chance to say anything else, I cut across the room. Someone stops me and says "great show." Someone else asks when the pieces will be on sale. I'm answering as graciously as I can but cut it short and hustle over to the entrance.

"I hope you're both talking about how great the show was." Lady looks away and my dad looks like he's ready to run out of here. "What? What is it?"

"The regular," my dad says. "I turned you against your mom, I don't know how to be a good parent, oh, and I shouldn't have made you move out on your own and definitely shouldn't let Kayla live with you."

My dad's glare is burning holes through Lady right now.

"And you know I'm right about everything I said."

"Really, Lady? This is what you came here for? To argue with my dad?"

"No, I actually came here to talk to you."

"Okay, well, make it quick. I have a whole bunch of people I should be talking to instead of you."

Lady asks if we can step outside so she doesn't have to talk over the music. When we get outside, I fold my arms and wait for her to speak.

"You are so much like your mother and you don't even recognize it." There's some joy in Lady's tone when she says this. "I know she would've loved to see how you grew up."

I'm not budging. I glance back inside and hope Lady gets the message.

"Okay," she says. "Let me get to the point." Lady reaches into her handbag and pulls out a small, purple box wrapped in a green bow. "I have something for you." Lady opens the box herself and lifts up the necklace. "This belongs to you."

I see my initials shifting side to side like the hand on one of those super old-school grandfather clocks. It's like I'm descending into a trance and whatever pain is shooting through my heart right now is telling me I should turn around and walk back inside.

"Why do you have this?" I still can't peel my attention away from the necklace.

"Never mind why I have it. It's yours. I want you to have it. Your mother wanted you to have it. And I know the story. Your mother cried when she told me how she took it away from you. You didn't deserve that, so I want you to have it back."

"Why? Why does it matter? You told me all about the family tradition or whatever, but I haven't been part of the family for years. Why do you care?"

"For someone so intelligent, I don't know why you can't understand. This isn't just about you, it's about family and tradition. It's about what the necklace represents. I keep telling you that nothing's more important than family. Nothing. This necklace is our legacy as women in this family. It's your turn to continue the tradition."

Lady's still holding the necklace in the air as she's speaking. She moves in closer to me and I instinctively lift my braids and let her wrap the necklace around my neck.

"Beautiful," she says. We both reach for the initials and our hands touch. I look at Lady for what feels like the first time and she squeezes my hand tighter. My head sinks into her shoulder and the tears flood down.

WALKING HOME WILL TAKE CLOSE TO AN HOUR BUT
I don't care. I'm already halfway there and I've needed every
minute of this walk to figure myself out. I sent Kayla home
in an Uber and she already texted me to let me know she's
there. Me, Derrick, and Jes made plans to go out after the
show, but I told them to go alone. Jes would normally force me
out, but she knows how to read the room so she bear-hugged
me and told me a million more times how proud she was.

My dad wasn't letting me walk all that way alone, so he's
right beside me, though he hasn't said a word the entire time.
My fingers have been caressing this necklace for almost every
step. I can't believe this thing is actually on my neck again and
I have no urge to tear it off or choke myself with it. When my
mom ripped it off my neck, it felt like a guillotine. When Lady
put it on me, it felt like a hug. And I know that's weird because
normally when you feel relief, it's supposed to feel like something's been lifted off your being. But that's not what happened.

Lady said it's the energy of over a hundred years of bold
women, women whose blood I share and whose commit-
ment to family made it possible for me to be here.

"All of our powers are in that necklace. That's what you're feeling right now," she said.

What am I feeling right now?

"I can't believe how great your show turned out." What other icebreakers did my dad think of before landing on that one? "You sold half your art pieces and you said you were already getting orders for your line, right? So incredible."

It was incredible. After that scene with my grandmother, I pulled myself together long enough to hear everyone tell me how much they enjoyed the show and loved the art pieces. I had to force my mind from wandering back to what happened with Lady, but I got through it. But when everyone left, it was like they took all my energy with them.

"What do you think, Coi?" Hearing my dad's voice feels like waking up from a dream.

"What do I think about what?"

"About doing another show? You have to. This one was so good."

I spot a bench beside the entrance of Trinity Bellwoods park and take a break.

"Were we ever really a family, Dad?" I wait for him to start chewing the inside of his lip, but he's quick to answer my question.

"What's your definition of a family?"

"I don't know. I mean, I know, but . . . It's like people say blood shouldn't matter when it comes to family but it totally does. The blood is the family I don't get to choose. The blood is the womb I floated in for months before popping out covered in it. But then I think . . . the only thing that really connected me to my mother was blood. If it wasn't for that . . ."

192

The streetlamps across Queen Street light up the trees in front of us. I can hear a streetcar skating through its tracks even though my back is to the road.

"My answer is yes, Coi. Yes, we were a family. For a while, your mom and I were all the family you had. When we moved into Elaine's basement together, we told each other it was us against the world. Nobody in, nobody out is what we'd say. We loved each other. As much as two teenagers can be in love, that was us."

"And you messed that up."

"We messed it up, Coi. Me and Crissy. We didn't realize how hard it was to be in a relationship. We just didn't know and we kept hurting each other."

"But you hurt her first and you hurt her the deepest because she never let it go. And why should she?"

I stare out at the park, not wanting to see the expression on my dad's face. The last time me and my dad were at Bellwoods together was for an art market. At least a hundred vendors filled this park with paintings, jewelry, candles, clothing and whatever other kind of art you can think of. It's where I found the photo of a young girl rowing down a river that hangs in my living room right now.

"That's not fair, Coi." My dad's voice breaks into my memories of happier times. "You can't blame me for what your mother did to you. I did everything I could to pull you out of that situation." He raises his voice. "I've dedicated my entire adulthood to you. Don't act like those mistakes define who I am. They don't. I'm not that person anymore."

I stiffen as his voice gets louder. It's hard to believe my dad is yelling.

"And," he continues, "you need to learn how to get over stuff too. Not for anyone else, but for yourself. So you can let go of whatever's keeping you this angry."

"I'm not angry."

"Yes, you are." His voice softens. "And I get why you feel like that but you need to be you, Coi. I know you think your mom was a nightmare, and she was. I'm not gonna argue about that. But you survived it. You're here. You graduated high school without a single grade under ninety. You make enough money from graphic design that you don't need a nine-to-five job. You just launched a freaking fashion line and you're still eighteen. I think you're doing okay. You have a lot to be thankful for. Seriously."

My dad sees me revving up a rebuttal and he puts his hand up to stop me.

"No, Coi. This isn't a debate. I've chosen to give you a lot of space to figure your own stuff out, but this isn't one of those times. I need you to listen to me and trust that what I'm telling you is the truth."

"CAN YOU TELL ME NOW?" KAYLA ASKS. IT'S THE day after the excitement and anxiety of my fashion show and I'm letting it all out on this run. Kayla's still breathing heavily even though we only ran half of my normal distance. We're walking slowly now, and it's early enough that only a few joggers are out so the path is clear and quiet enough to hear the short waves from the lake rise and fall.

"Let's go sit over there," I say. Sitting on top of the stones that overlook the water has been my new therapy. I've been out here nearly every morning since I moved. The stones are man-made and not nearly as high as a real cliff, but from where I sit, I can look out on the lake and see nothing but water with lights from the city brightening its edges. "You wanna know why I left, right?"

Kayla nods her head. This is the first time she's seen this view up close.

"Well, the first thing you need to know is that I didn't leave. Not voluntarily. Mom threw me out."

"Why?"

"What did she tell you?"

"Nothing. I was like nine years old. She didn't tell me anything. I just heard you guys fighting like you always did and when you left and didn't come back, I didn't know what to think."

I guess it does make sense. Even if Kayla was older, I doubt my mom would have offered an explanation.

"Did you ever ask?"

"I did, and she said you didn't wanna be there anymore."

Kayla turns away and stares into the lake. It's a bright morning, and the glitter from the sun looks like shimmering gold ornaments dancing in the water.

"That part is kinda true, but not in the way you probably think."

"Just tell me, Coi. I'm a teenager now. I can handle it."

She's right, and I know that, but it's not why I'm hesitating. Reliving these moments in my dreams is one thing. They're traumatic and feel as real as anything else, then I wake up and they're just memories like any other in my head. But Kayla's my sister. She's a part of me, a part of me that until this summer I've seen less than a handful of times in the last five years. For so long, she's been a memory, too. Except I couldn't just wake up and push this memory to the side. Not seeing Kayla, not speaking to her for all these years stays with me every time I open my eyes. It's what I imagine it's like for a wife to wake up without her partner after fifty years of marriage because that partner passed away.

"I remember looking back at you through the window, Kayla. Something told me I might never see you again. Like I felt it in that moment, know what I mean? You remember that? Seeing me leave?"

196

"Yeah."

"What you didn't see before that was what happened at school. It was Mom's week to pick me up but I asked my dad to come get me."

"Why?"

"Because the day before, I made my dad ask her if I could stay with him for a few more days. She didn't even answer his text. She just called my phone and started screaming at me. She said so many fucked-up things. She called me an ungrateful bitch and said that I didn't belong in her family. She said she wished my dad was dead so I would be alone and not have anyone."

I take a deep breath and lift my face to the breeze off the lake. The breeze is one of the big reasons I wanted to live by the water. Some people don't like it, especially in the spring after we've spent months in wool socks and parkas. But there's something about the way it hits my face that makes me feel alive.

"She really said that?"

"Yeah, and worse. Then she hung up, so I wasn't sure if she was actually coming to pick me up the next day. My dad agreed to come just in case my mom wasn't there, but when she pulled up to the school and saw him sitting in his car, she lost it."

Kayla rolls her eyes and gives me that look. We both know what it meant when my mom went off.

"How bad?"

"By the time I got outside, she was screaming at my dad through his car window, even though it was rolled up. As soon as she saw me, she stormed over and grabbed my shirt collar. I tried pushing her off but you know Mom."

"She grabbed you outside? In front of everyone?"

"Yeah, all my friends. A bunch of teachers and parents were watching, too. It was so embarrassing, but in the moment I was just really angry. Then Mom pushed me into her car. Like really pushed. And when my dad saw that, he came running over and they started screaming at each other again."

I should be able to smile while telling this story. Enough time has passed that my hands shouldn't be shaking. I shouldn't need to be counting to three in my mind while I'm talking to Kayla so I don't start hyperventilating.

"Then what happened?"

"I ran to my dad's car. No way I wanted to go home with Mom after that. But then she ran to my dad's car, too, and started yelling at me to get out. By then, there was a big crowd and my dad knew Mom wasn't gonna let up, so he got beside me in the back seat and told me to go with my mom. 'Trust me,' he said. So I did, and I let Mom take me home."

There's a scene in the *Batman* movie, the one where Heath Ledger plays the Joker, where the Joker is riding in a car with his head out the window. The scene is completely silent, but watching it, you feel this strange sense of anxiety and eeriness that runs through your body. That car ride back with my mom had that same kind of feeling. She didn't turn the radio on, she wasn't on speaker phone loud-talking with one of her friends, she didn't say anything to me.

"When we got back to the house, that's when she told me to pack up my stuff."

I'm not sure what kind of reaction I'm expecting from Kayla. I know she said she's ready to hear all of this but is she really?

"Why did she tell you to leave after she forced you to come home with her?"

"I don't know." And I really don't. "I think on the car ride home she made a decision. She and my dad were in the middle of a custody battle at the time and I'm guessing that that was a lot to deal with. Maybe she was fed up or tired or . . ."

"Or maybe she realized you didn't love her."

Kayla's not staring at the lake anymore. She's looking right into me like she's taking an X-ray of my emotions.

"That's not fair. Mom abused me, Kayla. Like she beat the shit outta me and called me names and made me feel like I hated myself. There's nothing I did to deserve that. And I did love her, but I wanted to be as far away from her as possible."

"Even if it meant being as far away from me as possible?"

"I didn't make that choice, Mom did. I was younger than you are now when Mom walked me out to my dad. It's not like I could've run away on my own."

Kayla squeezes her lips together. I can't pretend to know what she felt like losing her big sister so suddenly and without any kind of explanation. I reach out to hold her hand and we lock fingers.

"I'm here now, sis," I say. "And I'm not going anywhere this time."

The breeze is picking up and causing dents in the water. Two small sailboats are off in the distance, both with white masts catching the wind. We stay locked for a few moments without saying anything, but there's something I need to know.

"What was it like when I left?" Should I even be asking this? Do I really want to know? "Did anything change?"

"Everything changed." This is the first smile I've seen from Kayla since we started talking. "Mom wasn't much better to me when you were there, but when you left, she was different."

"Different how? Like, she didn't hit you anymore?"

"Nope. There was this one time I broke her sunglasses by accident, and when she saw me holding the glasses split in two, she grabbed me and raised her hand back like she was about to slap me. I closed my eyes and put both my arms up to defend myself, but she never swung. When I opened my eyes she was just staring at me. Then she let me go and walked away."

"And nothing after that?"

"She still screamed and whatever, but never hit me again."

There's a look of pride on Kayla's face and I get it. She's thinking of our mom right now but the mom she's thinking about isn't the one I knew. My memories aren't hers, and I know every sibling can say that to some extent, but this is different. There's a version of my mother I never got to experience, and even though that reality should soften the stone that's been around my heart, I stand up, turn away from the lake and start jogging again.

"Let's go," I say. "Keep up."

"WHAT ARE WE DOING TODAY?" KAYLA ASKS ME this every morning while we sit on the couch drinking tea or eating a slice of avocado toast, which is about all either of us can manage to eat before noon.

"I have a meeting with a client at two, and I'm working on doing a quick pop-up show before the summer's officially over. Or maybe just at the beginning of fall. Still figuring it out. But we can do something later this evening. What you have in mind?" After spending the last couple months with Kayla, I can always tell when she's hesitant to ask me something.

"My dad wants me to come home for dinner. I want you to come with me."

"To your dad's house?" Which is my mom's house. My old home. My response came out a bit aggressive and I can see Kayla already backing down. "I mean, why do you want me to come? Dave wants to see you, not me. You should go by yourself."

Kayla still has that hesitant look on her face.

"Our house is different now. Dad changed up a lot of stuff, some of it when Mom was still alive but most of it over the last few months. It's not the same. It's not like what you remember."

All that apprehension is through the window and Kayla is looking straight at me when she says this. And I'm looking at her, flashing back to when she was still crawling under tables and mumbling sounds meant to be words. Kayla's first sensible word was "uh-oh." I tried to make her drink from a regular cup instead of a sippy cup, and when the juice spilled all over her, she said, "uh-oh." Mom was right there when it happened, and we both laughed that entire day and for a few weeks after that every time Kayla said it.

"What time you wanna go?"

"Whenever. Doesn't matter. Whenever you're done working."

I don't have the same cynical premonition I did before going to the barbecue, but I still take a quarter of an edible cookie before we leave. Dave is cool so I'm not expecting any kind of battle, at least not with him. I'm more worried about stepping into that house again. Kayla might be right about the house not being the same, but that's just architecture. That house almost broke me, and I'm wondering what kind of spirits are still lingering under that roof.

Dave offers to pick us up but we decide on an Uber and pull up in the late evening. We drove past the plaza that my mom sent me to so many times to buy chewing gum and Zig-Zags. I saw my middle school, the yard empty but full of so many recess memories. Stepping outside the Uber, I trace the walk I never thought I'd take again. The four wide steps to get into the townhouse complex, the parking garage to the right with walkways and slimmer staircases on both sides.

As we walk up the front steps, small boys chase each other through a laneway. A group of young girls are sitting on a bench scrolling through their phones. No parents are outside, but I hear the voice of a mother yelling, "Shawn, grab your brother and get inside." My head feels light when I see the front door. There's a cool breeze this evening, but I stop walking and bend over when I feel beads of sweat pooling on my forehead and can't catch my breath.

"Are you okay?" Kayla's hand is on my back as I'm taking deep breaths.

"I will be. Just give me a minute."

The window is directly in my line of sight. The curtain is different, but I can still imagine Kayla's tiny head peeking out from inside.

"Do you want me to get my dad?"

"No, I'm good. Let's go."

I go to push the doorbell, but Kayla pulls out a key and opens the door. A couple pairs of sneakers are arranged carelessly on a thin mat, and the smell of oxtail and rice and peas heighten the nostalgia I've been feeling since I stepped onto the complex.

"My two favorite girls," Dave shouts from the kitchen. He's in basketball shorts and a red hoodie, shoveling food onto plates beside the stove. "You came just in time. Sit, sit."

The table isn't set and I remember Kayla telling me that they always eat on the couch while watching TV.

"You too grown to give me a hug, Coi?"

"Never."

All the window curtains are open and the lights are on, so even though it's gray and cloudy outside, inside feels like it's early afternoon.

"And this one over here," Dave says to Kayla. "I have to bribe you with dinner for you to come home? I see how it is."

Dave puts our plates in front of us and goes back to the kitchen to pour some carrot juice.

"I don't remember you ever cooking," I say. "Is this new?"

"Are you serious? I cooked all the time. You don't remember?"

"No way. Mom did all the cooking. At least that's how I remember it."

"Kayla, talk to your sister, please. She's losing her mind."

Kayla confirms that Dave did do a lot of the cooking and now I'm wondering why my mind blanked that out.

"You'll have to show her the vegetables in the backyard," Dave says to Kayla.

"You grow vegetables now?"

"Yeah, like three, four years now." Three or four years? That means my mom was still alive. I can't imagine her being patient enough to do any kind of gardening. "It was your mom's idea. I didn't wanna do it at first because I thought I'd get stuck doing most of the work. But she was out there every day till it was too cold to be out there. We had herbs the first year, then tomatoes and potatoes the second year. Now there's a bunch of stuff out there. We'll show you after we eat."

The backyard is through the dining room, which I can see if I turn around from where I'm sitting. It wasn't like this before. There was a wall closing in the kitchen that's not

204

there anymore. That's probably what Kayla was talking about when she said Dave made some changes. The floors in the living room are different, too. They're lighter colored. And this TV is much bigger than the one we had when I was still here, plus it's mounted on the wall instead of sitting on a TV stand.

Kayla is sitting on the floor with her legs crossed and Dave and I are on opposite sides of a narrow couch. The food smells delicious but my stomach feels queasy. I take sips of carrot juice and a small spoon of rice and peas with some potato salad. Kayla is lifting pieces of oxtail with her fingers and tossing them in her mouth.

"So," Dave says, "you actually came." My stomach is getting tighter even though Dave isn't threatening at all.

"I did."

"Does it feel weird being in here?"

"It does." He knows that. He has to. But he has that same face Kayla does when there's something else on her mind.

"I don't know what Kayla told you, but there's a reason I wanted you to come by today."

"You mean other than this oxtail?"

"Still a smart-ass, eh?" I am, but I'm also doing everything I can not to let Dave see my heart pounding out of my chest. "Thanks for taking Kayla. Let me just get that out of the way first."

"You don't have to thank . . ."

"Wait. Give me a minute. Let me finish first." I put my spoon down and lift my glass of carrot juice. "You know I grew up in a foster home. I never met my parents, so I don't know what it feels like to lose a parent because I feel like I never really had any. But you, you must feel like you lost your mother more than once."

I knew it would be something when I came over here. I'm not sure this is what I expected, though. Dave wipes his mouth with a paper towel and keeps going.

"And, you know, when I think about it, I should've done more for you. I always tried to stay out of whatever you and your mother had going on, but I should've done more."

"You're apologizing?" Suddenly the tightness loosens from my stomach and heat starts rising into my chest. "Now? You're really trying to apologize?"

"Coi . . ."

"Let me save you some time. I don't need your apology. I needed you to stop my mother from abusing me. I needed you to tell my mom that I was just a kid and not a bitch or stupid or a fucking babysitter before I had my period."

Dave puts both hands behind his head and leans back. Kayla's stopped eating and both of them are staring at me like I'm behind a fence in the zoo.

"Sorry," I say. "I didn't mean that. I mean, I didn't mean to say it like that. None of what my mom did is your fault. I shouldn't need defending from my mother, anyway."

"But you did," Dave says. "And I wasn't there for you. Not like I should've been."

I hate crying so much, but I've probably cried more times over the last few months than the five years before that combined. Not today, though. Not right now. I'm fighting these tears and finishing my dinner.

"Where did you get that?" Dave is eyeing my necklace.

"This?" It hasn't come off my neck since Lady put it on. "Lady gave it to me. Or gave it back to me, I should say."

Dave moves closer and inspects the necklace like he's trying to figure out if it's real.

"Wow, I thought this thing was lost. After Crissy passed away, I looked for it everywhere."

"My mom never told you that she gave it back to Lady?"

"No. I just thought she kept it after . . . you know."

"Yeah, I know."

I'm still fiddling with my food. Dave is back on his side of the couch doing the same.

"We're good, Dave." I say that without looking up. "I never looked at you as the villain. We're good."

Dave stands up and spreads his arms.

"Come get some of this. You know you want to."

I look at Kayla and she's covering her mouth from laughing, even as her eyes look shiny with tears. "You better give him a hug. He won't let you eat until you do."

I shake my head with fake exasperation and let Dave wrap his arms around me.

"Don't forget about me." Kayla stands up behind me and we're all embracing.

"Okay, that's enough," I say. "Get off of me. All this food is getting cold and this edible is kicking in so I'm ready to eat."

"YOU'RE REALLY NOT GOOD AT THIS GAME." IT'S THE fourth two- or three-letter word Derrick has played so far. "Scrabble just isn't your thing, D. You need help right now."

Jes just laid down "l-i-n-g-e-r" and added twenty-two points to her score. Kayla's a bit quieter than usual, but she and Jes are neck and neck so maybe she's just concentrating. She's my sister, which means she wants to win. Or it could be that this is her last week here, but I'm not exactly sure how she feels about that.

"I do need help," Derrick says. "I need you to tell me how you convinced my mom to let you stay in this apartment till the end of the year."

"Convince" is such a strong word. And to be real, it didn't take much convincing. I told Lucy I make enough money now to pay a bit more than $600, plus let her know how great it felt to be finding my way on my own. She was willing to let me stay even if I couldn't pay more; it was my dad who really took convincing. But once I told him it's basically like staying in a bourgeois dorm room, he loosened up.

"A lady never tells."

"No, seriously. What did you say?"

"Why you so pressed about it? You need to worry about spelling a word with more than three letters."

We're all in a circle on the floor with glasses of Cîroc in front of us along with a bowl of popcorn with way too much butter and a new-school R&B playlist running.

I let Kayla have one glass, and only a small glass. She said our mom's given her sips before but she doesn't really like it, which is every teenager's line when they're underaged.

"R-e-p-t-i-l-e," Kayla says. "That's seventeen points."

It's almost midnight but Derrick and Jes don't look like they're ready to stop anytime soon, so I pour another round of Cîroc (minus Kayla) and we keep the game going.

"Can I stay?" Kayla isn't looking at anyone when she says it, but I know what she's talking about. "I really like it here. And I know my dad won't mind. Or maybe he will. I don't know. But can I stay?"

Derrick is peering at me out of the corner of his eye and Jes is staring right at Kayla.

"You mean you wanna stay here a little bit longer?"

"No, I mean like . . . like stay here a lot longer. Like all the time."

"I don't know, Kayla. You start school next week and I'm not sure how your dad would feel about that. I mean, I get it. We had a lot of fun this summer, but it won't always be like that here."

"What if I get my dad to say yes? Then will you let me stay?"

Whenever Derrick asked me for a key, turning him down got easier every time because I was more sure the longer I lived on my own. But what do I say to this?

"I don't know, Kayla. I'm not sure that's a good idea." She's not in that window anymore. She's right here. My sister. My younger sister. And while I couldn't tell what she was thinking when she was peeking from behind that curtain, I can see all of her emotions right now as clear as my phone screen.

"You're right. Forget it. I don't even know why I asked." Kayla tosses her remaining letters onto the board and escapes toward the front door.

"Kayla, wait. Hey . . ."

"No. You don't want me here anymore. Cool. Couple months with me is enough, right? You did your part. Now you can disappear again."

"That's not fair, Kayla. I'm not gonna disappear." Kayla puts on her shoes and reaches for the front door. I grab her arm and she pulls away from me. "Kayla, it's midnight. You can't just leave."

"Leave me alone." Kayla pulls open the door, runs to the first staircase and pushes open that door. My first instinct is to run after her, but instead I watch the staircase door close slowly and walk back inside. Jes and Derrick are still sitting on the floor like they're watching a movie, and they might as well be.

"You're not gonna stop her?" Derrick says, and I ignore him. I walk to my room and grab a sweater.

"She doesn't need to stop her," Jes says to Derrick. "She already knows where she's going."

I'VE BEEN STANDING OUTSIDE OF THIS GRAVEYARD for at least ten minutes. I can see the small hills topped with reminders of lives lived and lost, and I tell myself that it's okay. That I can do this. That I need to do this.

The trail I'm staring into leads farther than I can see, and the darkness feels threatening, like I'll be swallowed up if I walk too far in.

One foot in front of the other, Coi. You can do this.

A few steps into the trail and I'm ready to turn back. I don't even know where my mom's grave is, but I know Kayla's here so I'm really focused on finding her. The first fork I reach is split by a large mound, and I decide to veer right without any idea of where I'm going.

"Kayla." How do I say her name loud enough for her to hear me but without waking up all the dead souls? "Kayla." Another fork and this time I go left. The deeper I slip into this cemetery, the harder it is for me to see, the more I have to think about my breathing and the faster my heart pumps. The flashlight from my phone is the only illumination, so every few seconds, I look up to find the moon. It's like a spotlight, and as I reach another fork, I feel so lost that my head feels light and I plop down on the ground.

The only thing that stops me from screaming is the thought of no one hearing me. This was a dumb idea. Kayla would've come back in the morning. I didn't have to do this. I didn't have to be out here besieged by bodies and dirt and darkness all by myself.

"Why are you sitting on the ground?" Kayla's voice sounds like it came from inside my head, but when I spin around, there she is.

"Kayla! Oh my God. Are you okay?"

"Are *you* okay? You're the one on the ground." Kayla reaches out her hand and pulls me up.

"I'm fine. I knew you were here. I just didn't know where Mom's grave was so I got kinda lost."

"You're not that lost. Her grave is right up here."

Kayla points to a single tombstone close enough that if it was daylight, I'd be able to read the words.

"That's her? That's Mom?"

"Yeah. You wanna go see her?" Kayla says it like she's asking me to go for a walk. I squint my eyes in the direction of the grave and don't say anything. "You're already here. Might as well."

I guess. Or I can just grab Kayla and leave and never come back here again. Or leave on my own and let Kayla do her thing. I haven't taken my eyes off the grave since Kayla pointed it out. It looks lonely, like a single tree without a forest, rooted to the ground with nothing else to let it know it exists.

But I can do this. Kayla walks over to the grave and motions for me to follow.

"Wait," I say. "Listen, I'm sorry about what I said back home. I really didn't know what to say and I'm not the greatest when I'm put on the spot. We can talk to your dad and figure something out. We're sisters, right?"

Kayla rushes into me so hard we almost fall to the ground.

"Thanks," she says. "You were always my favorite sister."

"You mean your only sister." We both giggle. "'K, you ready to do this?"

The few steps I take toward the grave are cautious, and when I'm close enough to see "Crissy Davis" engraved in all caps at the top of the tombstone, I fall to my knees.

"Mom." The sound struggles out of my mouth. Tears well in my eyes and a few drops escape into the earth beneath me. "Mom," I say again, this time covering my face. "I don't hate you, Mom. I don't hate you."

I touch the rise in the ground like I'm stroking my mother's hair. It feels softer than it should, like not all life has left it yet. With my eyes shut tight, I see my mother's face as clearly as I do in one of my dreams. We're standing at the top of a waterfall with our hands clasped, the water rushing swiftly but serenely under our feet. We're right up at the edge watching the water cascade to the bottom in peaceful explosions.

"Are you scared?" she asks.

"No," I say. "I'm not scared."

My mother looks at me one last time, smiles my smile, and lets go.

"BE CAREFUL WITH THAT BOX," I TELL MY DAD. "MY lights are in there."

"This is the last one right?"

"Yup, that's it."

Dad piles it onto the end of the moving truck then hops off.

"One last trip upstairs?" he says.

"Let's do it."

Nothing's left in my apartment except two plastic cups of tequila my dad was saving for this moment.

"Why does it seem like when you move, I'm the one doing most of the actual moving?"

"Because I'm your daughter and you love me."

"Uh-huh. That love is gonna start costing you."

It's still early enough in the fall that we only need our sweaters. Dad's sleeves are pulled up and he's sweating under his baseball cap.

"Well," he says, lifting his cup, "here's to another new beginning. And you're right, I do love you very much, daughter, and I'm proud of you. So proud of you. You've come a long way, Coi, and I'm happy to see where you've ended up. You're gonna be alright. Cheers."

We fling our heads back and swallow the shots.

"I told you don't make me cry. I'm trying to get through this dry-faced."

Back downstairs, we double-check that the movers have the right address before jumping in my dad's car. He just bought one last month — a hybrid Aviator that I'm only driving in for the second time. The first time was the day he picked it up. We cruised down Lake Shore and all the way up to Woodbridge, windows open the whole time. We blasted music and stopped for lunch at a fish and chips spot before he dropped me back to my apartment.

No music on this drive, though. The windows are cracked just enough to let the breeze through, and most of the trip will be on the highway. I text Kayla to let her know that I'm on my way and she texts back a row of heart emojis. I imagine her own heart fluttering when I told her that I'd be moving in with her and Dave. That happened less than a week after visiting my mom's grave and before Kayla started school. I haven't been back since, but that one experience released my emotions from whatever cage was keeping them captive. It was like I could see again, and what I saw was an opportunity for a family to heal together.

There's this saying that my mom made me memorize when Kayla was first born. I guess she thought I might get a bit jealous or feel left out, since Kayla would be getting so much of her attention. Every time I had a sour look on my face, she'd crouch beside me, lift my chin and instruct me to "say it out loud."

"First there was Daddy," I'd start, "then there was Mommy, then there was me, then there was Kayla, and then there was us."

"Good girl," she said with a kiss on the forehead. "And then there was us. Never forget that."

Epilogue

I KNEW WHEN I OPENED MY EYES THAT I'D BE BY myself. It's like I could feel her absence, like having a childhood friend suddenly move to another country. But blanketing those feelings of loss was the sight of the ocean softly crashing into the sand beneath my toes, the sound of the breeze brushing against the water's surface forming small waves that stretched as far as I could see.

My mother loved the water. She taught me how to swim before I reached kindergarten. There was a pool in the community center near the apartment we lived in after my mom and dad moved out of Elaine's basement. She'd pinch my nose and duck both of us under the water, then pop back up and shake her head back and forth to get the water off of her face. I'd mimic her headshake down to the exact number of turns. She'd shake her head again and watch me follow, then do it again, laughing every time I followed her lead.

I hear her laugh so clearly that I think she's right beside me, and maybe she is. But only my footprints are in the sand and I'm okay with that. I need to be okay with that.

"This is my dream," I say out loud. My voice echoes through the mountains that look closer than they really are. "This is my dream."

I sit down in the sand and squeeze my knees against my chest. The mountains tilt closer, like I'm about to tell a secret they don't want to miss, but there's nothing left for me to say. That's a lie. There's plenty I could say, plenty I could've said. As happy as my real life has been since moving in with Dave and Kayla, I still have days when I wish I could go back. I mean all the way back. Before I had control of anything. Would she be different?

That's the real question, isn't it? If I could go back, would anything be different? I can't even finish the thought without gritting my teeth.

"Stop it," I say to myself, and the mountains lean back into position.

Where would I be without these dreams? Seriously. Call it God, call it the Universe, call it whatever you want, but whatever it was that triggered those dreams changed my life forever. It gave us a chance, even though I thought there was no chance in hell I would ever speak to my mother again, much less forgive her. But here we are.

Dave says that he knew we'd end up back together, although he thought my mom would still be here. I don't believe him. Maybe he held onto hope for the first year, maybe the first two years, but there's no way he saw this coming. No way he saw me back in that house, especially if Mom was still there. The only reason I'm there is because she's not; that's the truth, no matter what Dave pretends to believe.

My dream shifts sharply and now I'm sitting in the middle of a highway. Cars and trucks are zipping past me while my knees are still tucked. Even though I can feel the pressure of each car speeding by, I don't panic. There's something peaceful about the chaos of the highway, some kind of order that makes me feel at ease. When I was nine or ten, I would count all the cars while I was on my way to school. I imagined what kind of life the people in each of those cars lived. Was that person rushing to work? How old was that kid in the back of the car? Why was that person driving alone?

I'm not sure I cared about the answers as much as I did about asking the questions. I was usually alone heading to school, so my mind wandered without distraction. Every day was a new set of cars, a new set of lives. I used to wish one of those cars would pick me up and take me somewhere else. Somewhere away from my mom. Now, sitting in the middle of the highway watching these cars go by, I sneak glimpses, hoping that one of them is carrying my mom.

When did I get this sentimental? Must be Kayla rubbing off on me. She's such a hopeful kid. Every time she talks, there's this excitement in her voice. It's almost like she thinks that she's been through the worst already, so she's going to make the best of everything from here on out.

My dream shifts again and now I'm nowhere. No ocean no mountains no highway; just me in a space with no light. I'm standing and waiting for something to appear, for someone to tap me on the shoulder or some of this darkness to be lifted. Minutes go by, then more minutes.

I'm hoping it's not hours before something happens in this dream. Not *this* dream, *my* dream. I almost forgot that part.

The darkness peels away as soon as I remember Jes's words. Familiar walls, a familiar face. My dad standing in the doorway of my bedroom in our first home on our own. If this was real life, he'd be telling me to come get some pancakes or maybe French toast. In this dream, though, he's just smiling and staring. It reminds me of when he dropped me off to Dave's house to move in.

I thought when I told my dad about moving to Dave's so I could be closer to Kayla that he would take it personally. The entire reason I moved out of his house, out of our home, was to be on my own. Then, less than a year later, I tell him I'm moving again and it's not to be back with him. That's a lot to deal with for a parent who was there for me every step of the way.

But as soon as I told him, he held both my hands and told me he was proud of me. He said I was doing the right thing and he knew I was changing Kayla's life forever. He also made me promise that I would see him at least once a week, a promise I've been more than happy to keep. On the day he dropped me off, though, after helping me bring my stuff inside, he stared at me the same way he is in this dream right now and smiled like I was boarding an airplane with no return ticket.

Back in my dream, my dad leaves my room and the only thing left is me. I'm on the same bed I was on when I heard my mom was in an accident, the same bed I was in when these dreams first started. I'm facing the window looking out at nothing in particular, except I know exactly what's out there. I know because I've experienced so many parts of life already. I'm ready for the surprise, prepared for the disappointments, anxious for the moments of joy and happiness that I know will eventually be tamed by some kind of pain. But that's okay. That's life. And I've made up my mind that nothing's ever going to stop me from living.